Praise for Marjory
DREADM

"Those who enjoyed Harry Potter but who seek a feisty,
determined female protagonist will find much to appreciate in
the complexity and atmosphere of Dreadmarrow Thief."
D. Donovan, Senior Reviewer, Midwest Book Review

"A novel that celebrates life and love
the way only the best fantasy tales can."
Kirkus Reviews

"A cracking adventure of discovery for all three of them...
A book that could be read as a standalone but I am very
fascinated to see where it will take me next."
Susan Hampson, Books from Dusk till Dawn

"The quest narrative is exciting and compelling...
a work of classic fantasy."
The Booklife Prize

"A gripping fantasy adventure.
A BRONZE MEDAL WINNER and highly recommended."
The Wishing Shelf Book Awards

"An epic quest takes three young people on an
unforgettable adventure... this book is wonderful."
Desert Rose Book Reviews

LAST GIRL STANDING

Marjory Kaptanoglu

First Edition March 2019

Copyright © Marjory Kaptanoglu
Published: March 2019 by
The Book Reality Experience

ISBN: 978-0-6484471-4-6
Paperback Edition

Cover design Luke Buxton | www.lukebuxton.com

To the four men at the center of my world:
my husband Sinan
and sons Tanner, Alan, and Derek

"Life is infinitely stranger than anything which the
mind of man could invent."
-Sir Arthur Conan Doyle, *A Case of Identity*

Chapter One

T he *Los Patos Water Company is determined to poison us.* Mom's words, not mine. She'd been saying it for so long, I still hesitated to drink the tap water. Even though no one in town had ever died of it, so far as I knew.

Feeling rebellious, I bent my head, ready to slurp from the faucet, when I glimpsed Mom's narrowed eyes watching me in the mirror. I changed my mind; it wasn't worth a shouting match. Instead, I splashed the water on my face as if I'd meant to do that all along. She continued down the hall, rebellion squelched before it began.

Dashing back to my room because I was running late as usual, I kicked aside the clothes on the floor to find my school books. I shoved them into my backpack, grabbed my cell, and raced to the kitchen. There I gulped a glass of filtered river water while Mom spread her homemade organic strawberry preserves on top of a slice of her homemade organic fifty-grain bread. Okay, maybe it wasn't fifty, but I lost count after ten.

She handed the toast to me. It tasted delicious, though sometimes I longed for a shiny sugary Pop-Tart, decorated with sprinkles the color of nothing you would ever find in nature, like my friend Giselle got to eat on a daily basis.

Mom twirled in front of me, modeling her outfit as she sometimes did when it was something new. "Do you like it, Sierra?"

I hadn't noticed the knitted whatever-it-was until now, because I was used to her looking pretty strange. At first, I thought she was wearing a blanket, but on closer inspection, it was a sort of fuzzy, purple/pink cape with armholes. "Um, nice," I managed to say, despite thinking it would take an apocalypse to get me to wear anything like it.

"I'm bringing it to Jane's Originals to see if they'll carry it."

"Good luck with that." I tried not to sound sarcastic as I shoved down the last bite of my toast.

She gripped my arm as I started to move past her. "Don't forget the water."

Of course I had forgotten the water. I usually hauled up a couple of buckets at the end of the day, but Mom had let me stay out past dinner the night before, on condition that I do my water shift before school.

"I'm late," I said.

But she just gave me the look that meant *you do this now, or there'll be trouble later*. She didn't care if I missed half of calculus, my first period class. Mom did not understand the value of any math beyond basic arithmetic. If my first class had been *How to Use a Spinning Wheel*, she would've prodded me out of bed an hour ago to be certain I didn't miss a second of that essential instruction.

I've known for some time that our family's not normal. It's just Mom and me and the hens and our goat, Brisa. Mom's an organic farmer and certifiable kook who would've fit in much better in the seventeenth century, before any modern conveniences were invented. According to her, we should all just grow our own food, find our own water, make our own clothes, build our own houses, and mind our own business. Well, maybe she would be willing to barter for some of those things she couldn't do herself.

Given her way of thinking, it was understandable she didn't trust water coming out of a tap. She posted this quote from Ian E. Stephens right next to our filter, to serve as a constant reminder of why we had to kill ourselves schlepping water from the river. The quote said, "Repeated doses of infinitesimal amounts of fluoride will in time reduce an individual's power to resist domination by slowly poisoning and narcotizing a certain area of the brain and will thus make him submissive to the will of those who wish to govern him." In other words, my mother believed water treated with fluoride could brainwash people.

We also had a rainwater collector behind the house, but so far we were having a dry winter and it hadn't rained in three weeks. Which was why I flung my backpack down on the chair, grabbed the clean water bucket, and rushed out the back door headed to the river.

The leaves were slippery due to being so dry, and as I hurried down the path, I suddenly found my feet shooting out from under me. *Crap.* I landed hard on my butt. I wasn't hurt, except for my self-esteem, but when I got up and tried to brush off the back of my pants, I realized I'd have to change them. *Great day to wear white.*

First I needed to get the water, because knowing me I was probably in for another fall before I made it back. In general, I was a klutz, and once or twice I'd even accidentally dunked myself in the river. Luckily the water didn't flow too hard in this section, and I was a good swimmer. But I wasn't taking any more chances today. I slowed as I reached the river bank.

The acacia tree across the water was in full display, its yellow flowers fluorescent in the dappled shade. I couldn't help but pause for a moment longer to take in the natural beauty of where we lived. The sound of the rushing river, the scent of the acacia blooms, the reflection of leaves in the silvery water where it pooled by the opposite shore… you'd have to be made of stone not to be moved by all this.

But calculus waited for no one, not even me with the best grade in the class so far. I swung the bucket into the water.

I saw it then. Ten yards upstream, a beige cloth or bag or something, caught on a short branch sticking out from one of the trees at the edge of the water. I was tempted to ignore it, but Mom had trained me too well about keeping the river clean. Especially if it might be plastic, I needed to fish it out. I put down my bucket and found a long stick—there was no shortage of them. Then I made my way along the river's edge till I was parallel with the floating thing.

A powerful stench, like a cross between a soiled diaper and rotting meat, clogged my nostrils and made me gag. I held my breath and spat, figuring the wind must've shifted and delivered the foul odor from somewhere across the river.

It was one more reason to hurry up and get out of there. I reached my stick over and snagged it on what definitely looked like clothing now, giving it a pull. The object rolled over, helped by the flowing water.

Something white and bloated and disgusting rose to the surface. Two eyes bulged and a tongue stuck out from what I realized must be the grotesque remains of a face.

My mouth dropped open and my breath caught in my throat. I tingled all over with pinpricks of dread. Then a shrill sound pierced my ears and I realized it was me screaming.

Chapter Two

Seconds after I screamed, Mom raced outside, letting the back door slam shut behind her. She probably pictured me being swept away by the current, or carried off by an abductor, or just plain getting myself killed somehow. Mom always imagined the worst, and this time she wasn't too far off.

Hanging onto the stick that still held the corpse, I managed to get out my cell with my left hand and call 9-1-1.

The dispatcher, a woman, picked up right away. "Nine-one-one operator. What is your emergency?"

"There's a body in the river," I shouted.

"Where are you?"

The question took me by surprise. Didn't she know? *Google knows.*

"I need your address," she reminded me.

"607 Sunset Drive." I said it fast. My right hand was starting to cramp.

"Again?"

I groaned and repeated it more slowly.

"What's your name?" she said.

"Sierra Mendez. I'm barely holding on with a stick!"

"Are you in any danger?"

"I'm fine, just afraid he'll sink if I let go."

"Help is on the way. Don't hang up."

The stick slipped in my hand, and I had to pocket my phone to get a two-handed grip. This all felt like a whole lot of responsibility laid on my seventeen-year-old shoulders, but with luck a cop car was only minutes away.

Then Mom fell like I did on the slippery leaves and slid down the trail till she landed at my feet. "Dang!" she cried out, knocking into me, making me stumble. My right arm jerked and the corpse detached from the stick, drifting downstream.

"It's moving!" I screamed, sounding like this was *The Walking Dead* instead of just the floating dead.

"My ankle!" Mom screamed back.

I made sure she wasn't about to fall into the river before taking off after the body. Her ankle would have to wait for emergency services.

Unfortunately, our small section of beach was the only part open to the water. Downriver, you ran into thick bramble, the kind that pokes through your clothing and doesn't let go.

I tried tromping down the brush and smacking it with my stick. Looking back at the water, I saw the body had caught on something again. Here was my chance to reel it back in, if I could only reach it in time.

"I think I broke my frickin' ankle," Mom shouted. "And what's that horrible smell?"

"The police are on their way!" I didn't have time to get out my phone and tell the operator to send an ambulance too. Chances were good at least one ambulance would show up anyway, or if not, there would definitely be a fire truck or two, and they always seemed to have EMTs with them. Our town was normally such a quiet place, whenever an actual emergency occurred, everyone wanted to get in on the action.

Mom would survive a sprained or broken ankle. But a dead man—or woman—adrift from family and friends, seconds from sinking before anyone could find out who they were… the thought decked me like a fierce kick to the chest. My father had also died alone.

Which made me all the more determined to reach the body. I lunged for it with my stick, but I was too late, the current had hold of it again. The corpse was sucked back toward the center of the river, where white foam gathered over it. When I could no longer see it, I dropped the piece of wood, knelt down, and hung my head.

Chapter Three

When I finally made it to school it was midway into third period. Mrs. Flanders was at the whiteboard writing down dates and the events that corresponded with them. I never understood why she didn't just use PowerPoint so she could put things down once and have done with it, but she was about two hundred years old and definitely old-school.

I took my seat in the back next to my best friend, Giselle, who was dying to know why I was late. We started whispering while Mrs. Flanders' back was turned.

"I found a dead body floating down the river," I said.

"What?!" Giselle said. Oddly, Mrs. Flanders didn't seem to hear. She just kept writing while her lips moved like she was talking to herself. More surprisingly, our classmates didn't appear to notice Giselle's outburst either. They were dutifully copying down all that Mrs. Flanders wrote. I couldn't remember everyone doing that before. I figured maybe our teacher had threatened to check all the notebooks at the end of class and give F's to anyone with a blank page. Because usually the way we did it was, one or two of us would secretly take a picture of the board and then email it to the rest of the group.

"Who was it?" Giselle hissed at me, clearly not worried about her grade. "Was it Mr. Delmar?" she added, without waiting for my reply.

"Rachel's father? Why would you ask that?" Rachel, a shy and serious student, was seated in the front row of our classroom.

"He's been missing since the day before yesterday," Giselle said.

"I don't know who it was. The body sunk. The cops were searching for it when I left."

"It must've been him." Giselle stared at the back of Rachel's head. "Oh god, that's awful. Are you sure he was—?"

The door to our classroom opened, and our principal, Mr. Meena, stepped inside. Normally he would smile at everyone, but today for some reason his eyes were glazed over and he looked bored. "Rachel, could you come to my office please?" he said. Twice he squeezed his eyes shut in a weird way.

Though Giselle and I exchanged a horrified glance, Rachel looked placid as she rose and followed the principal out. I expected her departure to be accompanied by the usual sort of *oooh, Rachel's in trouble* cracks, but none of the students looked at her. They just kept writing down the contents of the board.

Mrs. Flanders paused and I thought she was going to say something. Instead, acting as if a student had not just been taken from her class, she poured water from a pitcher into her cup and drank it down. When she finished, her face twitched sideways like she had some sort of nervous tic. She turned back to the board.

"Damn, I hope it's not her father," I whispered to Giselle. "I feel so bad for her."

"No kidding," Giselle said.

Another thought occurred to me. "Isn't he the water district manager?"

Giselle shrugged.

He was, though. I remembered now. He came to our house after someone reported our pump. It's illegal to pump water from the river without a permit, and Mom had neglected to get one, probably because she figured they wouldn't grant her one for no reason better than *you're poisoning us with the chemicals you put in the public water supply.*

"He gave Mom a big fine after coming to our house to remove the pump," I said. "She was so pissed." I was pissed too. That was when my daily trips hauling a bucket of water up from the river began.

Giselle looked at me. "I hope the cops don't think it's weird his body turned up at your house."

"Are you kidding me?" I knew she read a lot of murder mysteries, but this was ridiculous. "Mom wasn't that pissed. All she did was write him a bunch of letters."

"Threatening letters?" Giselle said.

I stared at her. I didn't know how threatening the letters might be; she hadn't shown them to me. But Mom could sound pretty crazy at times, especially when someone crossed her. I hoped there weren't any problems at home right now. The EMT had wrapped her ankle and told her it was most likely just a mild sprain. I had left her on the couch with her leg raised on a pillow, and a bag of frozen peas resting on her ankle. She had a book, snacks, and water on the table beside her. If she had any sense—which she didn't—she would not go outside to talk to any of the cops or rescue personnel who had swarmed our river access. Anyway, by now they ought to have moved further downstream in search of the body.

The bell mercifully rang and we got up to leave. Giselle and I raced to the door as usual. Normally everyone else raced there too, and we would all get stuck trying to push our way through a clogged drain. But today for some reason, the other students formed a neat line and followed us into the hall in eerie silence. It had to be a joke. I expected one of them to laugh out loud any second.

But no one did.

Chapter Four

It was lunch period after history. I went outside long enough to wolf down the sandwich Mom had made for me: cheese provided by our goat Brisa, lettuce and tomatoes from our garden, more multigrain bread. If nuclear war happened tomorrow, our place would be the most sought-after location in town.

After eating, I went to see if I could track down my calc teacher, Mrs. Suarez, who usually had lunch in her classroom. I followed my nose, tracking the coconut scent of the Thai curry she ate almost every day, despite that she was Venezuelan. On second thought, that wasn't really so strange. I loved Greek food, despite being American and Salvadoran.

I wasn't sure why Mrs. Suarez never ate with the other teachers, but she was usually doing something on her computer. Maybe when you're surrounded by a classroom of unruly students all day long, it feels good to have some solitary time.

She told me to come in when I knocked on the door.

"Sorry I missed class," I said. "I had an excuse for being late." I didn't really want to get into the whole dead body thing with her.

She gave me a vacant look and said nothing.

"Can I get the assignment?" I knew I could ask one of my class-mates, but I was hoping she would talk a little about today's lesson so I wouldn't miss anything.

She pointed at the whiteboard, where she'd written the assignment down. I sat and began copying it into my notebook. "Anything I should know from class today?" I said.

She stared blankly. "No, just do the homework." She blinked her eyes hard in that funny way I'd seen Mr. Meena do earlier, before draining half her water glass.

I wondered if she was pissed at me for missing class, and I decided I needed to tell her my excuse. "I found a dead body in the river," I said. "That's why I was late this morning."

"Oh," she said, sounding as interested as if I'd told her I'd gotten my teeth cleaned at the dentist's.

"Okay, well, I've got work to do," I said idiotically, raising my notebook. I hurried out of her classroom and nearly collided with my friend Myles in the corridor.

He grabbed my shoulders, which made my stomach flutter because we'd been hanging out for the last month and I was hoping things were finally starting to heat up between us. I think I even raised my chin a little, like my instincts were preparing for a kiss to be on the way. But then he just peered into my eyes.

"What're you doing?" I said.

"You look normal," he said.

"What's that supposed to mean?"

"You haven't noticed?"

I realized then he was talking about our classmates being the most boring version of themselves today.

"Everyone's acting weird, even the teachers," he said. "How could you not notice?" His eyes darted down the corridor at some kid I didn't know coming out of a classroom. The kid twitched his head sideways just as Mrs. Flanders had done.

"See!" Myles said.

"Just because he has a tic—"

"Everyone's got a tic today! Except you and me." He looked at me again. "What's different about us?"

"Giselle seems normal."

"Okay, one more. What's different about the three of us?"

"Maybe it's act-like-a-zombie day, and we didn't get the memo."

He seemed to actually consider the idea. "I just got back from camping with my dads last night."

"They took you out of school?" I was jealous.

"Hey, it was educational." He smiled, showing the one-sided dimple on his sculpted Asian-Caucasian face.

"You're coming to Giselle's tonight, right?" I said. She was having a small party in honor of her parents going out of town this weekend. I had texted Myles about it the day before.

"Yeah, I think so." His voice didn't carry a lot of enthusiasm, but then he perked up. "Wanna get lunch at Tacos Locos tomorrow?"

"Sure." I brightened. It might not be dinner, but it still felt like a date.

"Got some geometry I need your help with," he added.

Crap. Now it wasn't a date. Worse, it fed my fear that his interest in me was all about my math skills. It might've been okay if I thought the tutoring wouldn't last long. But whenever I helped him, I ended up doing all the problems myself, with him totally not getting it.

The bell rang. "Pay attention in class," he said. "Tell me I'm not right about everyone acting messed up." Myles hurried off.

I turned down the corridor toward my locker. As students poured in, heading to class, I watched their faces. A chill crept up my spine as I realized just how right Myles was. Everyone had a vacant stare. No one even made eye contact with me. Quite a few showed some kind of facial tic.

What the hell is happening? I whipped out my phone and texted Giselle: *Is this April 20?* She'd know I was referring to National Weed Day.

Her reply came back fast. *Yeah right? WTF?*

I was about to respond when an urgent text arrived from Mom: *COME HOME RIGHT NOW!!!*

Chapter Five

I tried calling Mom and texting her back, but she didn't respond. She was a dinosaur when it came to technology. Her cell was the only computer she owned, and she barely knew how to turn it on. I'd talked her into buying phones for both of us when I started high school, arguing that it would allow her to keep close tabs on my health and safety. After two and a half years, she still hadn't installed a single app. She was so bad at using her phone, she often accidentally shut off the sound so it didn't ring or buzz when calls or texts came in. And without any noise to remind her, she never thought to check messages on her phone at all.

So I had no choice but to jump on my bike and ride as fast as I could back home. Her use of ALL CAPS was strange. She didn't usually send messages in all caps, although she often sent comically misspelled and auto-corrected messages with caps and no caps mixed randomly together. This sudden and unexpected coherence on her part made me fear that matters at home had taken a turn for the worse. First there was Mom's ankle, which hadn't looked too bad, but she was known for her lack of common sense, and she might've tried to do something that could've caused further damage. Second and more importantly, there was the dead body, which could very well turn out to be a man Mom threatened both publicly and privately. Maybe someone from the police had shown up to question her.

Twenty minutes later I rode up to the carport, where Mom's pickup was still parked. Her bike was also in its usual place, so she had to be home, unless she'd been silly enough to hobble somewhere on that ankle. Turning to the house, I was surprised to see the front door left wide open, but I reminded myself Mom often left it ajar, even on normal days. I hurried inside, calling out her name. She was not on the couch where I'd left her, and she didn't respond to my shouts. I dashed into the other rooms in case she'd passed out somewhere, but she was nowhere to be found.

I paused and tried calling her cell again. A second later came her annoying ringtone that sounded like crickets. I followed the sound to a place behind the couch, where Mom's phone lay on the floor.

I was seriously worried now. *Is she kidnapped?* Whoa, I needed to slow my brain down. I hadn't even checked outside yet.

Heading out the back door, I scanned the area by the river. *The river.* What if she'd gone down there again for some bizarre reason, fallen on her bum ankle, and plunged straight into the water? She was a strong swimmer normally, but her wounded joint could cripple her.

I rushed down to the riverside and stared at the water. Well, obviously, if she *had* fallen in, she wouldn't still be hanging around here. I began to look along the shore for any sign that she had been there recently. I'm not sure what I was thinking… maybe a strand of purple thread from the cape she'd been wearing? It was all too Sherlockian for me.

I didn't really think she'd try to walk far with a painful, swollen ankle. She was such an odd bird she didn't have any real friends in town, except for Owen who came over sometimes. I didn't have his number, so I trudged back up to the house to call him from her phone.

"Hi sexy," he answered.

Ew, I thought. "This is Sierra," I said right away to avoid any more *sexy* talk. "Have you seen my mom lately?"

"Man, I wish. Mendocino is trippin'."

"You're in Mendocino?"

"Didn't she tell you?" Like this was *New York Times*-worthy news. "Workin' on my next sculpture for Burning Man."

"Have you spoken to her today?"

"No, I been beachcombin'. Lookin' for driftwood."

"Okay, never mind."

"Everything all right?"

"Yeah, it's nothing," I said. Owen wasn't exactly the type you could rely on in an emergency, even when he was right here in town. "Have fun."

"I found this cool—"

I hung up. There was no time now to listen to Owen's description of his latest Burning Man creation. I called 9-1-1 and the dispatcher—whose voice I recognized as the same one who'd shouted at me in the morning—now sounded just as out of it as everyone at school. I told her about my missing mother and she asked me to hold on. A minute later she returned and said, "Your mother is at the downtown station."

"What? You're kidding." Despite my worries of her being suspect number one, I didn't think anyone would go so far as to bring her to the station.

"I'm not kidding," the dispatcher said.

"Why is she there? Let me talk to her."

The dispatcher hung up on me. *Karma, I guess.* I took Mom's phone and mine, grabbed the keys to the truck, and raced out. *Can this day get any worse?*

Chapter Six

I never liked driving Mom's ancient pickup at the best of times, but it was harder than ever to keep the thing under control while breaking all speed limits on my way to the police station. Swerving into a right turn too fast, I accidentally careened into the opposite lane. Luckily the car coming toward me was one of those self-driving Zipis that started appearing all over town a few months ago, and it darted out of my path instantly. I have to say, although it was super weird at first, overall the Zipis seemed to perform a lot better than your typical human, who always had some sort of distraction going on, whether it was texting, or rocking out to loud music, or eating a hamburger. Still, it was freaky to see a totally empty car scoot by when it was on its way to pick someone up. At least when there was a passenger, you could imagine you were in the UK and the driver was on that side.

I screeched into the police station lot, turned into a parking space, and slammed on the brakes. As I jumped out of the truck, I noticed an officer walking toward his cruiser. I was afraid he might cite me for reckless driving, but he didn't even look my way. I hurried on past him, went into the station, and approached the front desk.

"I'm here for Lauren Woodard," I said matter-of-factly, trying to act casual like of course they'd be bringing her right out for me.

Officer Barrera—whose name I read on her badge—sat staring at her computer. I gave her a minute but she still didn't look up. "Excuse me," I said. "I'm here to pick up Lauren Woodard."

Finally the officer glanced at me. "Woodard?" she said in a mono-tone.

"W-O-O-D-A-R-D." I wanted to give the impression of being helpful.

She typed the name on her computer. "Ms. Woodard is here for questioning," she said after a minute.

"I know, but isn't she done by now?"

"Captain Leach will speak to you." Officer Barrera's hand twitched on her keyboard.

A man came out from the back section of the station and walked up behind the officer. Though dressed in full uniform, he didn't look anything like a cop. More like the grown-up version of Josh Wilson, who was number two in my calculus class. Both were medium height and pudgy, with splotchy skin and crooked glasses.

"*Help me, Captain Leach, you're my only hope,*" he said in a high-pitched tone like he was imitating a woman.

"Excuse me?" I said, completely baffled.

"Leia? *Star Wars?* 'Help me, Obi-wan, you're my only hope.' Ha, always wanted to say that. I'm Captain Leach, chief of police." The man now spoke in a nasal whine, presumably his normal voice.

I was stunned into silence, which was not something that happened often. A geeky, *Star Wars* quoting police captain? Not only that, but I was pretty sure our chief of police had been African-American and Captain Leach was pasty white. This guy must've replaced him pretty recently. To top it all off, he was eyeing me in a most unhealthy man-ner, considering he looked about forty, and I'm seventeen. "I'm Sierra Mendez," I said. "I'm looking for my mother, Lauren Woodard."

He raised his eyes from my cleavage. "Let's continue in my office."

Despite my misgivings regarding what it was he thought we might need to continue, I followed him down the corridor and into his office. My stomach clenched when he closed the door behind us.

"Have a seat." He turned to the counter and poured a glass of water from a pitcher.

The one chair aside from his was next to the strangest thing I ever saw: a life-sized Lego sculpture in progress. Enough of the structure was done to tell it was Gollum lifting the One Ring in triumph after having bitten Frodo's finger off.

Captain Leach caught my gaze. "Amazing, huh? Wasn't easy to transport. I've been working on it for a year."

I did not ask what a police captain was doing building a giant Lego sculpture in his office. This had to be the weirdest police chief we ever had, and we'd had a couple doozies, at least according to Mom.

He handed me the water. "Drink up." It sounded like a command.

I sat down in the chair, balancing the glass in my lap. He took his seat behind the desk.

"I'd just like to speak to my mother," I said. "Lauren Woodard." I wasn't sure how many times I'd have to repeat her name before I got anyone to take me seriously.

"Uh," he said. "Not possible."

"Why not?"

"After she refused to answer our questions, we put her in a cell."

"She's in a *cell*?" I couldn't believe how fast things were happening. "Did you charge her with something?"

"Not yet," he said. "We're thinking about it."

This had to be the most unprofessional police chief ever. "Then I don't see how you can keep her there," I said. If he'd been a normal police chief, I don't think I'd have dared to speak so openly. Because he had such a whiny, adolescent quality, I felt emboldened.

"Uh, yes we can."

"Did you let her call a lawyer?"

He didn't answer. Instead, he picked up a piece of paper on his desk and read from it. "'I would love to take the pump hose and wrap it around your scrawny neck.'" The captain looked up at me. "One of the many choice lines your mother emailed to the man who drowned outside your house. Mr. Delmar, the water district manager. We found his body, by the way."

"He didn't drown outside our house! He just happened to be floating by." It was a *river*. The body could've come from anywhere. "And the emails didn't mean anything. She was just upset."

"Upset enough to kill the man?" He noticed a stray Lego that had been under the paper and picked it up.

"How can you say that? She's not going to commit murder over a stupid water pump."

"Her letters weren't just about the pump. She accuses him of poisoning everyone in town."

"If you would just let me talk to her…"

He stood and brought the Lego over to the sculpture. "When she cooperates," he said. "Not before. Now finish your water."

Despite Mom's warnings, I did occasionally drink tap water. But I didn't much like the taste, and I liked Captain Leach's insistence even less. I pretended to fumble with the glass as I stood up, letting the water spill out onto the floor. "Oops, sorry," I said.

Captain Leach walked over next to me. "Thank you for coming," he said. He placed his hand on my lower back, and by that, I mean upper ass territory, and pushed me toward the door. At the same time, he bent his head and hissed into my ear: "Don't fuck with me, little girl."

The hair lifted on the back of my neck. I'd just been threatened by the chief of police.

Chapter Seven

When I reached my truck, I just sat for a minute, trying to sort through everything that had happened today. *The town's gone mad,* was all I could think. From a floating body, to strangely distracted teachers and classmates, to Mom getting arrested, to a sinister new police chief… where would the craziness end?

There had to be explanations for all this, but in the meantime, Mom needed my help. I had to find her a lawyer. My friend Ben's mother was a lawyer, but I didn't know what kind. Could a patent attorney give advice on a possible murder case? Still, if she turned out not to be the sort of lawyer who could take on Mom's defense, she might know someone to recommend. That sounded better than my doing a Google search and just picking some loser at random.

I had texted Ben earlier to let him know I wouldn't be showing up at his place for our usual after school video game marathon. He hadn't replied, which was pretty unusual for him. His house wasn't far from the police station, so I figured I might as well drive there and hope for the best. When I pulled up out front, I noticed the garage door wasn't open like it generally was. Ben's father, who was a handyman and took care of the kids, liked to spend a lot of time outdoors with Ben and his two younger brothers. They played basketball, kicked the soccer ball around, and sometimes even worked on the front garden. But no one was outside today.

I texted Ben again to let him know I was at the door. When there was still no reply after a minute, I rang the doorbell. I had to ring it two more times before Ben finally opened it. He stared blankly at me. His normally alert blue eyes had a dull sheen, and even his blond, young-Seth-Rogen-style jewfro—as he called it—was matted down and unusually subdued.

"Didn't you get my texts?" I said.

"Yeah," he said.

"Um, okay. Hey, I was wondering if I could talk to your mother about a legal thing." I'd decided not to confide in Ben. I didn't want everyone in town knowing Mom had been arrested. She had enough of a reputation already, and this could hurt her business. She was a regular at the farmer's market with all her food and clothing products.

To my surprise, Ben showed no curiosity. "Come in," he said, moving back to let me pass. "She's in the family room."

I followed Ben into the house. Sure enough, his entire family was gathered around the TV in the family room. No one looked up when we entered.

"Mom, Sierra wants to talk to you," Ben said.

Mrs. Schwartz, who had the same hair as Ben only longer and tamed with hairspray, slowly turned her head toward me. "All right," she said. She waited for me to speak.

"Um, privately?" I said.

She seemed reluctant to tear herself from the TV as she stood up and walked toward me. "This way," she said. She led me to a home office and shut the door behind us. She neither sat nor offered me a seat.

I quickly explained the problem.

"I'm an estate attorney," she said when I finished. "I can't help you."

"Can you recommend someone?" I said.

"No," she said. Then she left the room, leaving me standing there feeling stupid.

I knew then that whatever crazy virus was sweeping the town, this family was infected. I returned to the family room, where all the Schwartzes were again seated, quietly watching television. They snacked from a bowl of popcorn on the table, and sipped water in between bites.

I'd never seen anyone so intent on watching a show, except when it was the Super Bowl. But this was some sort of local infomercial, with its message apparently being repeated in a loop. I watched while it started again.

An attractive woman gestured before photos of how our town— Los Patos in the middle of nowhere—was about to be transformed into an oasis. Thanks to a new federal grant and the generous support of Pardize—a company that had recently completed a vast new research facility in the midst of the parched wasteland along our town's southern border—Los Patos would soon be in a position to provide free food and medical care to all our residents, and housing to those who didn't already have it. Photo after photo showed dirt lots transformed into community gardens and fields of wildflowers, condemned housing turned into immaculate residences and shiny office buildings, and transients replaced by healthy, smiling, well-groomed homeowners. The pictured residents spanned the spectrum of diversity when it came to race, skin color, size, physical ability, sexual orientation, and gender identification. All were welcome in this big new wonderful Land of Oz.

This was the first I'd heard of it, and the plan smelled fishy to me. That the entire zonked-out Schwartz family seemed to be swallowing it hook, line, and sinker, just made it fishier.

Chapter Eight

It was past six when I arrived back home. The first thing I did was look up defense attorneys in Los Patos. There weren't a lot; a testament to our town having nothing of any real value that might attract the criminal element. I ranked the lawyers by Yelp rating, but it didn't matter, because eventually I called all of them without once reaching a single live person. I guess if you're caught breaking the law after six pm, you better be prepared to spend the night in jail.

At this point I was starving and figured I should eat something. My stomach couldn't bear to wait for anything to cook, so I made a plate of fresh vegetables and Mom's bread, with hummus and nut butter for dipping and spreading. I ate that down fast, then fetched a couple of oranges from our tree. This time of year, they were as sweet and juicy as they ever got. Maybe because I was feeling bad about Mom, it occurred to me I really ought to appreciate her a lot more than I did. Though I craved junk food now and then, I really did love all the fresh, homemade goodies provided by my mother, and I knew it was healthier for me too.

I poured myself some filtered river water. Just as I lifted the glass to my lips, Mr. Delmar's bloated dead face flashed into my mind. *He was in the same river.* I had fetched this batch earlier, but then... I didn't know how long he'd been drifting around. I began to wonder just how many dead animals might be at the bottom of the river I'd been drinking from all my life. Strangely, I'd never really considered it before.

I frowned at our filtration system, wondering just how effective it was. I didn't think it could compare to the filtering method used by the water district. I'd probably be much better off drinking out of the tap.

But then I thought of Mom and how miserable she must feel tonight, stuck in a cold, cramped jail cell. It would seem like a betrayal to start drinking the tap water now, right after she'd been yanked out of our home. If I was going to switch, I should do so honestly, to her face, letting her know I was an adult (or close enough) and would be making my own choices from here on out. Until that moment... I would respect her rules.

So I chugged down the river water and gagged a bit at the end, unable to keep the image of poor Mr. Delmar out of my head. I left the kitchen quickly, hoping to distract myself with my calc homework. I sat down in the family room with the book in my lap and stared at the page. However, my mind insisted on drifting to my father. *Dear Papá.* He would've known what to do to help Mom.

Tears sprang to my eyes as I thought about him. The memory brought with it the odor of sickly, fake-buttery popcorn. Day and night, Frank's Food Market had served up fresh popcorn to its customers. I can't smell it without my thoughts spiraling back there.

I was six years old and knew better than to steal anything. But after my father told me I couldn't have the Snickers bar, I snuck it into my pocket. As soon as we got home, I ran into my room to eat it.

Papá, suspecting something was up, had followed me without my hearing him. "What you got there?" He spoke with a melodic Spanish accent in a voice that still caressed like velvet inside my head.

I tried to hide the candy under my leg. "Nothing," I said.

"C'mon," he said. "Let me see it."

My face burned as I drew it out to show him.

"We didn't pay for that, Sierra."

I nodded my head in shame. The theft had been spur of the moment, and now, terribly regretted.

He reached out his hand. "I know you won't do it again. But we need to go back and pay for it."

I gave him the Snickers without looking at him and followed him out to the car like we were headed to a funeral. My funeral.

Mr. Franks, the owner, greeted us with a sour face.

"My daughter has something to tell you," Papá said. He gave me a gentle push forward.

I did as he'd coached me on the way over. "I'm sorry, Mr. Franks," I whispered. "Here's the money for the Snickers I took." I held out a five-dollar bill with a trembling hand.

He snatched it from me and rang up the purchase. As he handed my father the change, he said, "Your family is no longer welcome here."

"Excuse me?" My father looked stunned.

"You heard me."

"She's a child. We came here and—"

"We have a strict policy about this. Anyone caught stealing is banned from the store."

"No one gets a second chance?" Papá's voice was loud, attracting looks from other customers.

"Don't make me call the police," Mr. Franks said.

"The police? What the hell are you talking about, man?" Papá was shouting now, and he looked scary to my childish eyes. Maybe he looked scary to Mr. Franks too. My father was taller and younger than him, and his muscles bulged under his shirt sleeves.

Mr. Franks raised his phone.

"We're leaving," Papá said. "I wouldn't be caught dead shopping in this piece of crap store." Then under his breath he added, "Asshole."

I could tell Mr. Franks heard him from the way his face twisted all up. It sent shivers right through me. Even at the tender age of six, I knew there were going to be consequences.

Chapter Nine

I snapped my calculus book shut. Homework wasn't happening right now, that was for sure. A distraction was needed, otherwise I would go crazy waiting to hear from Mom. I figured I might as well go to Giselle's house for the party. If they let my mother go, she could call my cell from the station and I'd pick her up immediately.

I drove the truck, resolving to have no more than one beer and then I'd still be okay for fetching Mom, or driving home if I didn't hear from her.

Giselle lived on top of a hill overlooking our town, in a house that resembled a castle, as if she was some kind of fairy princess. Several majestic oaks grew near her home, while vineyards covered the rest of the hill and the valley below. Her parents operated a winery, with the tasting room located a short distance from the house, so everything had to look perfect at all times. Basically any time of year you went to her house, there would be flowers blooming somewhere on the property.

Giselle, an only child like me, occupied the entire lower level of the house. She had an enormous bedroom, next to an equally enormous "playroom." Then came the "entertainment room" which had double doors leading to her own private patio outside. Talk about spoiled.

But my friend wasn't spoiled. She knew other people didn't live as she did. In a lot of ways, she wished she'd had a more normal life. She was like Rapunzel in her tower, always looking for ways to get down and hang out with regular people.

I parked near the front porch, right next to a huge new shipment of bottled water that some delivery person had dumped in the driveway. Clearly the Prices weren't about to drink out of the tap, with all the money they had. Still, they ought to know better than to create all that plastic waste. I made a mental note to talk to Giselle about it after the party.

Continuing around back to the patio, I knocked on the double doors. Giselle came right away and let me in. When I saw her, I wished I'd spent more time fixing myself up before coming here. I was in jeans and a T, while she had on a sexy new dress that showed off every curve she had. The yellow color was a great choice to contrast her black hair and brown skin. Though her father was white, Giselle had inherited the characteristics of her stunning African-American mother. Normally I didn't begrudge my friend her great looks, but after all the horrible things that had happened today, I silently cursed myself for not trying harder to find a best friend who was less hot than me.

"No one's here yet," she said. After having convinced her parents she was old enough and mature enough to be left home alone for the weekend, the first thing she did was plan a party. I guess it just goes to show you can't trust a seventeen-year-old.

There was a keg on the deck, pizzas on the coffee table, and chips, Cheetos, and Doritos in bowls everywhere else. Giselle opened the fridge (yes, she had her own fridge down here) to show me it was stocked with water, soda, more beer, and five bottles of the family's premium chardonnay. On the table beside the fridge, red liquid in a punch bowl had ice cubes bobbing inside it. "What's that?" I said.

Giselle laughed. "My parents would die if they knew I mixed their award-winning cabernet with ice and fruit punch."

Yeah, I thought, *they'd die all right*. I knew her parents and how they were about their wine. Her mother was the winemaker and had won a bunch of awards. Her father, the more gregarious one, handled the business end and frequently greeted visitors in the tasting room.

Giselle started blasting her playlist, an odd mix of rap, pop country, and indie rock. We each filled a solo cup with beer from the keg and threw ourselves on the couch to wait.

"Is Myles coming?" she said.

"I guess." He hadn't said for sure.

"Are you guys… you know…?"

I shrugged. "I'm helping him with geometry."

"You like him, though?"

"Well, yeah."

"I bet he's totally into you. He's just using math as an excuse to get closer," she said.

"You think he's that shy? He's like, one of the most popular kids at school."

"Because he's the star of the soccer team," she said, starting to sound peeved with me. She picked up the bowl of Cheetos. "Want some?"

I scooped up a handful.

"I've been meaning to tell you," she said, not making eye contact. "I've started seeing Randy."

My stomach twisted. "Randy?"

"Yeah. I like him. Amazing tats."

"I know." He and I had a history. We were good friends for a while, and then, a month ago, he asked me to a dance. That same afternoon, I ran into Myles and he invited me to dinner at Shake Shack. Every girl at school wanted to go out with him, and he had asked *me*, a geek who was home-schooled till ninth grade. How could I say no to that? I texted Randy that I was sick, but just my luck, he spotted us leaving the restaurant. His eyes had frozen up and he'd crossed the street to avoid us. Since then, we'd barely spoken.

I knew I'd done a shitty thing. The worst part was, things hadn't really gone anywhere with Myles, other than his math grade was improving. I missed hanging out with Randy.

It was clear Giselle wanted reassurance I wasn't still pining for him. I squeezed her hand. "I'm sure you guys will be great together." It gave me a lump in my throat to say that. But she was my best friend and besides, the Randy ship had sailed. He probably hated me now. I needed to make things work with Myles.

Another hour passed without anyone showing up. Giselle rose and looked outside for signs of headlights coming up the drive. "Nope," she called out.

As she walked back toward me, she looked close to tears. "Did I do something wrong? Why are all our friends ditching my party?"

"It's not you. Everyone was weird today. Maybe they're sick or something."

"Everyone?"

I shrugged. She sat down beside me and we got out our phones. I texted Myles. *We're at Giselle's where r u?* I peered at the display and saw there were no bars at the top. No service.

"You have trouble getting service here?" I couldn't remember that happening before at Giselle's house.

She looked up, her face confused. "Not usually." She tried making a call. After a minute she shook her head. Meanwhile I was attempting to get on the Internet, but no website would load. "Crap," I said.

We looked at each other like two wild she-lions suddenly deprived of our cubs. That was the level of despair we felt.

Giselle grabbed her TV remote and flicked it on. Netflix, Hulu, YouTube, and all those other places were not even listed anymore. She just had basic service.

It was set on that stupid new local channel that was advertising all the changes that would soon be happening in our town. Giselle flicked the channel, and it was the same thing. She kept going for twenty more channels… all the same. Throwing down the remote, she turned to me. Our eyes conveyed the depths of our mutual horror.

Chapter Ten

I'd only had one beer so I was fine for driving home. Giselle had wanted me to stay the night, but now that I knew my cell wasn't working, I needed to go home. If Mom did get a chance to call me from jail, she would have to call our landline. We actually had one due to Mom being a product of the Stone Age. She even said once, as a justification I guess, that if all the cell towers in California were blown to smithereens, our landline would still work.

And... I didn't mention it to Giselle, but I also wanted to check in on Myles. Though he was normal when I saw him at school, by now he might've joined the night of the living undead. That would explain why he hadn't come to the party. But just in case he was still okay and had a different reason for not showing up, I had to try to find him and warn him this thing might be catching.

I parked a few houses down from his and walked the rest of the way. It was only ten pm on a Friday night, but the neighborhood was supernaturally quiet. No cars driving down the street, no people walking outside. I didn't even hear any dogs barking.

I had to go through Myles' side gate to reach his bedroom window in the back. His dog knew me so I wasn't worried about that. Anyway, I didn't see her so she must've been inside. All the lights were out, making me wonder if the whole family had gone to a late dinner or movie or ice-skating. *Ice-skating?* I wasn't sure where that came from, other than Myles having two gay dads. God, I hoped I wasn't blithely dropping stereotype bombs like that when I talked to them.

Maybe he simply forgot about the party. That stung, since I still had hopes he saw me as more than a math tutor. Would I rather find out he was infected, or that he just didn't view me as girlfriend material? Weird that I couldn't quite make up my mind on that question.

I'd decided not to ring the doorbell in case his parents were sleeping and got pissed. You never knew when people of their generation went to bed. So instead I scraped up a few pebbles from the garden and began tossing them at Myles' window on the second floor. I'd been to his house a couple times and I was pretty sure it was that window.

I threw three pebbles one after the other, then paused to wait a bit. Nothing happened. The light didn't flick on and Myles didn't come to the window. I tried three more pebbles, a little larger than the last ones. Still nothing. Probably he wasn't even home. Deciding to give it one last attempt, I picked up something that in all truth, was more of a rock than a pebble, and flung it at the glass.

The window cracked. *Crap.* I looked around in case anyone heard it in another part of the house, and prepared to run.

Then I saw him. Myles. Standing at his window looking down at me.

He didn't look like himself. He was like the other kids at school today. Blank-faced. Hooded eyelids. While I watched, his face twitched sideways. Somehow, maybe because I was alone out there and it was dark, he looked sinister. A shudder ran through me.

I rushed away, back through the gate to the front. I raced to my truck three houses down on the dark street, feeling petrified that Myles might follow me. Myles. The guy I'd been hoping would be my boyfriend.

He was just like the others now. How much longer before I became one of them?

Chapter Eleven

This was one time I wished we lived on a busier street. We had no near neighbors and a long, winding driveway descending to our house by the river. Given how I was feeling at the moment, it was nerve-wracking. The only light came from my headlights. I was used to the glare of the spotlight outside our house when I came home at night, but silly me, I'd forgotten to turn it on.

As I drew closer, I saw a faint glow inside the house. It must've been from the front hall light, the only one I could remember having left on. Mom had trained me too well to save electricity. I pulled into the carport, shut off the headlights, and found myself plunged into total darkness. I turned the headlights back on, jumped out of the truck, and found the flashlight Mom kept on the shelf. After switching it on, I cut the headlights and got the keys.

On the path between the carport and the house, it felt like looming shadows closing in on me, though I knew they were just trees. The wind had picked up, creating crackling sounds that could've been footsteps. The overcast sky blocked any chance of moonlight relieving the oppressive darkness.

I hurried into the house, disturbed to find I'd forgotten to lock it on my way out. Clearly I was already losing my mind. A shiver ran through me as I stepped into the kitchen, listening for the sound of intruders. All was quiet—maybe *too* quiet. I bolted the door behind me.

Now I felt like I needed to check every room in case someone had snuck inside. Not that any of those blank-faced crazy people seemed to want to leave their own homes, but who knew if this disease might have a stage two? You know, like stage one: vacant-eyed robot, stage two: homicidal maniac, stage three: dead, stage four: undead.

I went into the family room and switched on the lamp nearest the door. Looking around, I noticed the message light blinking on our landline phone. I rushed over to it, thinking Mom must've called. Instead I got Owen singing *I Can't Get No Satisfaction* at the top of his lungs. I jabbed the *Delete* button as fast as I could, before confirming we still had a dial tone. At least now when the stage two psychotic killers showed up at my house, I would be able to call 9-1-1. This was important, because finding the dead body in the river this morning had taught me that none of the neighbors could hear me scream.

It chilled me to wonder if I could actually count on help from Captain Lech or any of his dazed minions.

I was tempted to get Brisa the goat and let her sleep in my room tonight, but unfortunately, she was extremely friendly and just wanted everyone to pet her. This was one of those times I really wished we had a German shepherd or maybe a pit bull. But Mom had never let me get a dog because she thought it would upset Brisa.

It would've been nice to check the news on TV, assuming there was something on besides the creepy advertisement. But television was another big no-no to Mom. No computers, no TV, no nothing. Just my phone, which still wasn't able to access the Internet. It was useless at the moment, except as something to hurl at a prowler's head.

I held my phone out for exactly that purpose as I crept up the stairs. I nearly freaked when I flipped the switch for the hall light and it didn't come on. Then I remembered the bulb was out and Mom had been planning to replace it today. From there, I rushed into each bedroom and the two bathrooms, turning on lights. My heart raced as I checked under the beds, inside the closets, and behind the shower curtains. At the end of my search I felt better, but still far from relaxed. A tap at my bedroom window caused my breath to catch, but when I peered out, I could see nothing but blackness. *It's just the wind,* I told my frazzled nerves.

I brushed my teeth and prepared for bed. Since there was zero chance of my sleeping at the moment, I went in search of a book. Thanks to no Internet, I couldn't download anything new. I was caught up on everything else I'd been reading, so I padded down the hall to check Mom's bedroom. Examining her bookshelf, I couldn't believe the macabre selection... Poe's stories, Anne Rice's vampire novels, and every horrifying thing Stephen King ever wrote. The covers were enough to terrify me.

This would not do. I returned to my own room and got into bed with my US History textbook. If that didn't put me to sleep, nothing else would. I turned to the section on one of our most boring presidents, Martin Van Buren, and started to read. Sure enough, it took no more than five minutes of his ineffective policies to cause my eyelids to droop.

That was when I heard it. The sound of someone rattling the front doorknob. I held my breath, feeling a tightening in my stomach. At the same time, I slowly lowered my book and set it to the side. My eyes searched the room for a better weapon than my phone.

The front door creaked like it was being opened. I gulped back air, struggling not to be heard, knowing I had to act quickly. I reached for the lamp and switched off my light, so its glow wouldn't draw the intruder to my room. Though my knees felt weak, I forced myself up, crept to my shelf, and grabbed my soccer trophy. Sadly, it was only for participation. I regretted not having put more effort into the team; I might've learned how to kick hard enough to get this asshole in the groin.

The trophy was lighter than I expected—*what was it made of, gilded plastic?*—but at least the base had some weight to it. I positioned myself behind my door, ready to strike.

The floor planks groaned on the first floor. There was a pause, as if the intruder was listening. A moment later a step sounded on the stairs. Followed by another. And another.

My hand shook as I raised the trophy above my head.

The quiet footsteps reached the second floor and continued toward my room. Through the crack in the door, I saw a dark shape approaching along the unlit hall.

I lunged out, prepared to strike. A woman cried out.

"Mom!" I shouted at the same time. Luckily I'd managed to stop myself in time. I threw the trophy to the side and wrapped my arms around her. "Mom, I could've killed you!" Even in the heat of the moment, I knew that was technically untrue. More likely the flimsy trophy would've broken into pieces, and Mom would've gotten no worse than a scratch.

She gave me a short pat on the back and lowered her arms. I let go and reached over to turn on my lamp.

"How did you get out of there?" It was strange, but I felt a flash of pride to think my mom could be badass enough to have broken out of jail.

"Captain Leach sent me home in a Zipi," she said, continuing down the hall to her own room.

I followed her in. "You took a Zipi?" Previously she had sworn she wouldn't get into one of those things as long as she lived. I presumed that meant her corpse could go for unlimited rides.

"Yes." She began taking off her clothes.

"So the charges are dropped? Everything's okay now with the cops?"

"Yes, everything is okay."

"Good. How's your ankle?"

"Fine. It doesn't hurt anymore." She put on her nightgown and picked up the cup by her bed.

"I'll fill it." I reached for the cup to bring it downstairs.

She didn't let go. "I'll do it." She walked to the bathroom, turned on the tap, and poured water into the cup. I stood there watching her with my mouth hanging open.

Then she drank the entire cup down.

I nearly fainted. *"Mom."* I could barely get out the word. *"You drank the tap water."*

When she turned toward me, her eyes blinked oddly three times. "Goodnight," she said, getting into bed and pulling the covers over her.

I returned to my room and sat down on my bed. My hands felt clammy. *Mom has the disease.* That much was clear. I stared at the glass of river water at my bedside.

It's the water. The revelation hit me like a metaphorical brick. All these years of Mom telling me the tap water was poisoning everyone… and now it seemed it really was.

Everywhere I'd been today, people had been guzzling water. My next thought made me gasp: it was the water district manager who had been murdered. What if he had been trying to keep the water pure? Pure for tap water, anyway.

The lecherous new chief of police had tried to force me to drink it. He hadn't appeared to be doped up himself. Maybe he was behind all this. Whatever "all this" was. I couldn't imagine why anyone would want to drug the residents of sleepy Los Patos.

Of the people I knew, only Giselle was still normal. *Her family drinks bottled water.*

I didn't think she minded tap water, though. What if she got up during the night, didn't want to fetch a bottle from the new stash outside, and drank from the faucet? She would be infected, and I would be utterly alone.

I couldn't take the chance. I had to warn her. *Now*.

Chapter Twelve

Before leaving to warn Giselle, I had the brilliant idea to turn off the water at the main valve outside. Then I went back into the house and drained the rest of the water out of the tap. If Mom's brain was as fuzzy as it appeared, she might assume the city cut our water and there was nothing we could do. I needed to keep her away from the tap for at least eight hours, in the hope that the drug or bacteria or whatever it was would leave her system and she'd be back to herself. Part of me couldn't wait to see her excitement when I told her she'd been right about the water all along. Clearly we were looking at something new here, and the water hadn't always been this way, but she'd been right about the *potential* for using the town water supply to drug everyone.

After taking one more glance at Mom, who looked like nothing short of a cyclone could wake her, I put my jeans, sweater, and Adidas back on, slipped downstairs, and grabbed my jacket along with the keys to the truck. Chances were excellent Mom wouldn't hear the engine starting up, or even if she did, she wouldn't have either the energy or the desire to do anything about it. I took my phone with me in case it started working again, but the way things had been going, I had no expectations of anything good happening.

Friday night at 11:45 pm. and I'd never seen the town so dead. Seriously. No cars driving on the streets. None. Even the Zipis were neatly parked in their designated spots, and though obviously the best option for keeping our roads safe from drunk drivers, no one was requesting them. Which was crazy because Friday and Saturday nights were usually prime time for all those planning to drink themselves senseless.

The houses I passed were mostly dark. A few places had left on a light or two, but there were no silhouettes at the windows to indicate anyone was awake. I lowered my driver's side window, curious to hear any noises, wondering if I might somehow come upon that one home in the neighborhood where everyone had gathered to party till they dropped. But there was nothing. No music blaring, no burst of sirens from a cop cruiser, not even any dogs barking. That last part made sense when I thought about it. After all, pets were drinking the same tap water their owners were. It must've lulled them into listlessness as well. No more defending the house. *Shoot my people and take what you want*, the apathetic dog would think as he rolled over on his other side. *Just don't wake me up.*

A feeling of utter isolation swept over me and made my hands grow damp on the steering wheel. What if Captain Lech—my name for our chief of police—was driving around and decided to pull me over? He might claim I was violating some new curfew. It might even be true. I wasn't sure if our town could legally set a curfew or not, but I wouldn't put it past our city council members to vote for something just because they could, and then not tell anyone about it. Especially now, with their brains turned to mush.

I turned onto a back road that would eventually connect with Giselle's street. Neither Captain Lech nor any of his officers were likely to be cruising this far from the main drag. But I had forgotten how poorly lit this lane was. Rich people lived here with their fancy homes set back from the road, and their driveways blocked by iron gates. You would think folks who owned stuff that was actually worth stealing would want to light up the area like it was Christmas in order to repel prowlers. But for some reason it was the opposite, and you couldn't find a street light to die for.

Ahh! A shape appeared in front of the car, coming out of nowhere. I slammed on the brakes and swerved sideways, my tires skidding. I wrestled with the steering, barely managing to avoid careening into a ditch. Braking lightly, I straightened the wheels, continuing forward. My hands trembled as I checked my mirrors, petrified that something might be following me. I didn't see any movement behind or to the sides, but considering how dark the road was, this didn't reassure me.

Whatever I saw had resembled a skeleton more than a person. Long bony limbs… bulging eyes… lipless teeth… I shivered thinking about it. What if I was wrong about the water being drugged, and instead it was a disease? What if there really was a stage two that would turn everyone into whatever that thing was?

No, I must not think about that and what it would mean for my poor mother. That was just a man who ran by, I told myself. A skinny, malformed man. He couldn't help looking the way he did.

He had been running across the street in the darkness. I'd seen it—*no, him*—when I was about to hit him; I probably missed him by an inch. Presumably he just kept running in the same direction, but my attention had been on the road ahead of me, so I didn't know.

I took slow, deep breaths, trying to calm myself. Focused on the way ahead of me, I repeated these thoughts inside my head: *Just get to Giselle's. Don't stop. Don't think. Don't look at the shadows along the side of the road.*

One thing was certain, I made the right choice coming out here to warn my friend. Minutes later, I turned onto her street and continued up toward her house. The driveway remained empty of cars. I parked in the same place as before and got out, looking furtively around in case Skeleton Man magically appeared behind me. The contents of my stomach lurched at the thought.

I hurried around to the side where Giselle's private entrance was. Her light was out; chances were she'd fallen asleep. I knocked on the glass and waited a minute, checking again for spooks behind my back. When she didn't come, I tried the door and found it unlocked.

That worried me, because Giselle was super-responsible, and I doubted she would leave the door open when her parents were out of town and she was alone. Especially given the events of the day, and the fact that her phone wasn't working.

I moved quietly into her entertainment salon. Everything looked pretty much as we'd left it. I had promised to help her put it all away tomorrow. I guess then we were still vaguely hopeful of rustling up a party Saturday afternoon. Now I knew we had zero hope of that.

The sound of a voice came from Giselle's bedroom. *Maybe Skeleton Man.* My eyes shot around the room looking for a weapon and stopped on an empty bottle of the award-winning cabernet she had poured into the punch bowl. I hurried over and picked it up, happy to discover it had a nice solid weight to it, in keeping with the quality of the wine, I guessed.

I tiptoed to the bedroom door and paused to listen. Over the din of my thumping heart, I heard rustling movements. I couldn't afford to wait any longer. I flung open the door and peered into the darkened bedroom. Two forms lay on the bed, one pressed over the other.

The man's assaulting her, I screamed inside my head, dashing into the room with my bottle raised.

Chapter Thirteen

The two forms on the bed sprang apart. "What the hell?" shouted Randy.

Oops. I dropped the wine bottle in mid-swing.

"What're you doing?!" Giselle said, turning on the bedside table lamp.

"Sorry!" I replied lamely. At least they weren't under the covers, and although Randy was shirtless, the rest of his clothing and Giselle's looked intact. I didn't believe they'd been doing the deed, though they might've been getting close. "There weren't any cars out front," I went on.

"Randy came by skateboard," said Giselle. I followed her eyes to where it lay on the floor by the wall.

I looked at her. "I thought you were being attacked."

"Seriously?"

Randy slumped at the edge of the bed and muttered to Giselle, "Didn't you say she went home for the night?"

"It was dark in here. I couldn't see," I said. Now that it was light, there was no mistaking the chiseled outline of Randy's arms and shoulder blades, and his smooth, coffee-colored skin. He kept his black hair very short on the sides, a little fuller on top. Mesmerizing tattoos—on his right shoulder, and around his left arm like a band—depicted mountains and clouds and ocean waves… earth, wind, and water. His tats, which he designed himself, showed the heavy influence of Japanese art.

Realizing I was staring, I jerked my eyes away. I didn't want either of them to think I still had feelings for him. It was clear he had none for me.

"Did something else happen?" Giselle said.

I collapsed onto the nearest chair. "Mom. They let her out of jail. She actually rode a Zipi home. And then…" My voice came out hoarse. "She drank the tap water."

Randy did a fake gasp.

"That's it?" Giselle said.

"You know how she is. There's something going on. I'm sure of it." I watched as they exchanged a look that said *her-mother's-crazy-gene-has-finally-kicked-in.* "I know what you're thinking," I continued. "Tie me up in a straightjacket, but I really believe something's been added to the water that's changing people. It's like they're drugged into just sitting around and not asking questions."

Neither one of them responded, but it looked like they were thinking about it.

"It hasn't gotten to us because I drink river water. Giselle drinks bottled water."

"What about Randy?" Giselle said. "He seems normal enough."

"Enough?" he said.

Giselle followed my gaze to an empty Gatorade bottle by the side of the bed.

"I'm betting that was his," I said.

Her face filled with understanding. "Gatorade. Soda. Juice. Man, do you ever drink plain water?" she said to Randy.

"It's tasteless," he said. "I need flavor."

"There you go," I said. "The three of us don't drink tap water, and we may be the only normal people left in town."

Randy frowned. "My grandmother is training for a triathlon. She just aged into a new category and thinks she has a chance to win against the geezers. Every day she's riding her bike, running the river trail, and doing laps at the Y. But not today. I get home and she's watching TV. Did you know our town is turning socialist? Like that would happen here, a place that voted for Trump."

I shot to my feet. "Someone's trying to take over our town. They killed the water district manager. They hired a nasty new chief of police."

Randy and Giselle's stares made me realize that was probably too much information at once. I resolved to leave out Skeleton Man for the time being.

"Take over Los Patos?" Giselle said.

"Who would care?" said Randy.

"Something's happening. We have to try to stop them. Whoever they are." I turned to Giselle. "Where exactly did your parents go?"

"Carmel for a golf tournament."

I took out my phone and tried for a signal again. *Nothing.* Giselle and Randy did the same.

"Shite," Giselle said. She was into British swears at the moment.

"That's it then," I said.

"That's what?" said Randy.

"We have to drive to Carmel."

"I'll get my clubs."

"I'm serious. We need help. Giselle's parents are probably not affected yet. We can't afford to wait. Someone might make us drink the water. They made my mom. They tried to make me."

Silence settled over us until Randy stood up. "Let's keep trying to call on the way there. If we manage to talk to them, we can turn back." He held out his hand. "I can drive first."

I dropped the keys in his palm. My stomach fluttered when my fingers accidentally brushed his skin, but I was sure that came of the uncertainty and fear surrounding our plan. That Randy, glancing up at me, seemed to sense something between us too, was only my imagination.

Chapter Fourteen

We filed out from Giselle's house together, and she locked the door behind us. Randy tossed his skateboard into the back of the pickup, then went around to the driver's seat. I slipped into the back, leaving Giselle to ride shotgun. It was going to be three or four hours to Carmel, and I hoped to get some sleep on the way.

"I need directions," said Randy, right after starting the ignition.

Since the truck had no GPS, Giselle and I pulled out our phones, having forgotten yet again that we weren't getting any signal. And sure enough, no signal.

"What're we going to do?" Giselle said with a plaintive edge, as if she'd already decided we had no hope of reaching Carmel now.

All of Mom's pronouncements seemed to be coming true today, like how she predicted my generation would be completely helpless if anything ever happened to interfere with our precious technology. And now, here we were, clueless about leaving town without our phones to guide us.

I got an idea. "Open the glove compartment," I told Giselle. "Mom might have some maps in there."

"Maps?" she said.

"A folded document that says 'California' on it." I couldn't believe I had to tell her what a map was. "It'll look old, like from the 1800's."

"I know what a map is. Just surprised you have any." Giselle rummaged in the compartment until she found it and handed it back to me. "You look at it," she said. "I suck at geography."

I carefully unfolded the map, which was torn along some of the creases, and shined my phone light on it. *At least that still works.* "Take 4 west," I said. "You need directions to the highway?"

"I can get out of my own town. I meant directions when we get near Carmel," said Randy.

I threw the map aside. "Fine. Wake me in an hour and I'll give you the next instructions then. Meanwhile you guys keep checking your phones, okay?"

"Where is everyone?" said Giselle, looking out her side window.

Randy was driving us through downtown, and it was as dead as the last time I'd seen it, about an hour earlier. We glanced from side to side, anxious to find any evidence of normality, but every place was closed, everyone gone… Los Patos could've been a ghost town.

When Giselle looked back at me, she had a glimmer of panic in her eyes. "You were right. We're the only ones not affected."

Randy turned at the light, following the signs toward the highway. Fewer street lamps lined the road in this section, and I was reminded of Skeleton Man bounding in front of my car. I decided it would be best to continue not mentioning him or they might really think I was crazy and begin to distrust everything I said. Even I was wondering if I'd lost my grip on reality and had only imagined that strange apparition.

"Hey," Randy said. "What's that light up ahead?"

I peered through the front windshield. Farther along, it looked like a spotlight had been placed in the middle of the road.

"Crap," I said, getting a bad feeling about this. "Maybe we should turn back."

But Randy kept on going, straight toward the light.

"Turn back, Randy," I said, louder than before. "Let's try a different route."

"Uh, I'm not sure there is one. Let's see what it is."

It had been a mistake to hand over the keys to my car. But now it was too late to turn back.

Three cop cruisers were parked in the road ahead of us. They'd set up the spotlight between them, and beyond that, a rudimentary barricade blocked the entrance to the highway. A police officer waved Randy over to the side.

My stomach tightened. "Don't tell them anything. We were just…"

"Going to visit Jason," Randy said, referring to his older brother. Jason lived in Stockton, about an hour's drive from Los Patos.

Randy pulled over and rolled down his window. The cop approached with a flashlight, which he proceeded to shine in all our eyes. He was young enough that he still had acne on his cheeks, and peach fuzz he was trying to pass off as a beard.

"Where you going?" The cop spoke in a flat voice, sounding like one of the stupefied. That was my new name for those who were dumbed down by whatever they were putting in the water.

"Don't answer that," Giselle said, making me want to kick her under the seat. Giselle planned to go to law school to become a criminal defense attorney, but she often talked like she'd already passed the bar exam. I loved that she cared so much about people and animals, but it could get tiring always having to do the right thing around her. "What's this blockade?" she added. "Why can't we go through?"

"Quarantine." The cop blinked twice.

We all exchanged horrified looks. "Uh, quarantine?" Randy said.

"What are we being quarantined for?" I said from the back.

"Plague," the cop said, in the same unconcerned tone he might use for "allergies" or "toenail fungus."

"*Plague?*" In many ways it seemed like we'd hopped into a time machine and propelled ourselves back into the middle ages. "Bubonic plague?" I said.

"Just plague. Turn your car around and go back."

"We really can't leave town?" Giselle said. "What about people trying to get back home?"

"It's a quarantine," he said. "Nobody goes in or out of Los Patos."

"But we're not sick," I added. "We want to get out. You can't make us stay here with all these sick people."

Another officer approached. "Is there a problem here, Broomfield?" His voice and the way his face jerked sideways told me he too was one of the stupefied.

"They aren't leaving, sir," the first cop said.

The new officer, who had gray hair and a hawk nose, stared at Randy.

"We're going to Stockton," Randy said. "To visit my brother."

"Go home," the officer said. "Nobody's going anywhere."

"Sir," Randy said. "We don't have the plague."

Hawk nose looked at the younger cop. "Take these kids down to the station." Peach Fuzz actually began to draw out his service revolver.

"We're leaving now," Randy said, starting up the engine.

The two cops backed away to make room for Randy to turn the car around. "Anyone who tries to break the quarantine," the older officer said, "will be shot on sight."

Somehow I knew the police would take these instructions to heart, despite their being stupefied. Or maybe because.

Chapter Fifteen

"What do we do now?" Giselle said.

We had driven back to her house, because at least there we would have the place to ourselves. Giselle was on the brink of a meltdown. "My parents won't be able to come home. I can't even call them."

"Wait," I said. "Do you guys have a landline?" We should've thought about that before heading out in the car.

She stared at me blankly like she was trying to remember what that was. "In the kitchen," she said at last.

Randy stayed behind while I followed her upstairs to the family kitchen, which was bigger than the entire downstairs of my house and filled with dazzling appliances that looked like they'd come off the factory line yesterday. A quaint, old-fashioned-looking phone sat in the far corner of the room. Probably, like ours, its main function was to field telemarketer calls. I was one hundred percent certain Giselle had never used it before.

On her cell, she looked up the contact number her parents had given her and dictated it to me. I dialed and handed the phone to her. She held it out so we could both hear as it rang twice and then delivered the following message: "During the current state of emergency in Los Patos, long distance service is unavailable. Please hang up and dial again if you wish to place a local call."

Giselle swore and slammed down the phone. We returned down-stairs to find Randy on the couch with the TV on. He muted the sound while Giselle paced in front of him, telling him about the phone call.

She paused and looked at me. "What if there is a plague? You think we're being poisoned by the water, but what if the plague just makes people thirsty? That's why everyone's guzzling water except us. We're immune or something."

I thought for a minute. "If it's the plague, it's the weirdest one ever. Physically, everyone seems healthy. It's their thinking that's messed up."

"Maybe it's a virus that attacks the brain. What do we know? We're not medical professionals."

"So why aren't they rounding up people and putting them in hospitals? My mother was in jail and they sent her home. To infect her daughter, I guess. It doesn't make sense."

Giselle grew silent again, probably trying to figure out how to counter me. As a future lawyer, she hated losing arguments.

Randy turned the volume back up and started surfing with the remote. Every channel showed the same thing: the infomercial about how Los Patos was about to be transformed into some kind of socialist mecca.

He pressed the pause button. "What about them?"

I sat down on the other end of the couch and stared at the image of the high-tech facility, newly completed, that was supporting the effort to transform our town into the progressive ideal of free food, housing, medical care, and education for all. The company name was emblazoned across the top of its massive new structure: PARDIZE.

"What is this place?" I said.

"How could you have missed it?" Giselle said. "Construction's been going on for two years. It's enormous."

"I know that." For god's sake, I would have to be blind and deaf never to have seen or heard of it. "But what exactly do they make?"

We all looked at each other blankly.

"I think they described it as, 'tech industry components,'" Randy said.

"Components?" I said. "Could be anything."

Giselle whipped out her cell. "I'll look them up…" Her face fell as she recalled that her phone was no more useful than a paperweight. "Dammit."

"You see?" I said. "That's why this isn't a plague. If it was, why would our access be cut off? Why would we have nothing but one station to watch on TV now? It's because someone's behind this. Someone doesn't want us to figure out what's going on. Someone doesn't want us communicating with the outside world. And the only clue as to who that someone might be is right there on your TV."

"Pardize," Randy said. "Sounds like Paradise."

"So what do we do?" said Giselle. "Just drive over there and ask them what the hell is going on? Are you making components or what? Are you drugging us? And just why is that?"

"Uh, no," Randy said. "If we start asking questions, all they have to do is force some water down our throats."

Randy shut off the TV. We all sat in silence for a few minutes, dazed by the implications of everything that had happened in the last twenty-four hours. A creepy, suffocating feeling settled over us as we threw glances toward the windows and doors. I shivered, wondering if our enemies might already be surrounding the house, ready to kidnap and drug us like the others.

"I'm tired," said Giselle.

Her words made me realize how exhausted I was. It had been a hell of a day. My phone showed the time as 2:15 am.—one other thing it was still good for.

56

"Can I sleep on your couch?" I said. At the moment, I couldn't face going home to a stupefied mother. I didn't believe she was in any danger, and there was a chance she'd even be back to normal in the morning since I'd cut off her tap water supply.

"Sure," said Giselle, giving Randy an awkward glance, making me wonder if she was expecting him to join her in bed again.

He made clear that wasn't happening by announcing he was going home to make sure his grandma was all right. I instantly thought of Skeleton Man.

"I'll drive you," I said.

"No thanks," he said, grabbing his board.

"C'mon. It isn't safe."

"She's right," Giselle said.

"I'll be fine." His hand was on the door.

"I saw a strange person running across the road earlier." I stopped short of calling him Skeleton Man.

"See you tomorrow," he said, going out.

We watched him hop on his board and maneuver along the walkway to the driveway. He was so skilled, the board was like an extension of his feet. I tried not to worry. If anyone could elude Skeleton Man, it was Randy on his skateboard.

"We might as well share my bed," Giselle said.

"Sorry," I said.

"What? No. I wasn't expecting him to... all I want to do is sleep."

I couldn't agree more. The problems—and there were many—would have to wait till morning.

Chapter Sixteen

Sunlight blazed inside Giselle's bedroom when I woke up, checked my phone, and found out I still had no service. I blew out air and with it, all my hopes that yesterday was a figment of my imagination or somebody's sick idea of a practical joke. This thing was real.

It was past noon. I wasn't sure how I'd managed to sleep so long, especially with all this dazzling light in here. It just showed how exhausting *crazy* could be.

Giselle made noises in the shower. When she was done and dressed, we ate some unhealthy sugar-saturated cereal for breakfast before heading out in separate cars. Her plan was to meet up with Randy at his apartment and try to find out how other people in town were doing. Mine was to go home, check on Mom, and figure out next steps based on her condition. Giselle gave me a key to her house, and we agreed to meet back there at the end of the day. It felt strange planning so much in advance, after being used to making instant decisions by text.

Today was Saturday. As I drove through town, I didn't think it looked as busy as a normal weekend, but it wasn't dead like the night before either. Shops and restaurants appeared to be open and cars passed me on the road. People were on the sidewalks and waiting for lights at intersections.

I slowed my speed, trying to get a close look at the pedestrians. Most were alone and intent on wherever they were going. No one smiled or acknowledged anyone in passing. Their faces twitched.

As desperately as I wanted the citizens of Los Patos to be normal, clearly they were still stupefied. But whatever drug they were getting, it didn't affect their ability to walk around and do things. They looked as if a hypnotist had told them: "You will go to the pharmacy at ten in the morning, get your prescription, and come back home the way you came. You will do nothing else, you will mind your own business, and you will not stop to speak to anyone." And everyone would follow the instructions exactly, without dawdling, without speaking, without allowing anything to distract them.

And so the nightmare continued. I accelerated towards home, starting to worry about Mom again. After parking in the carport, I hurried into the house through the kitchen door. A tiny flame of hope lit inside me on seeing Mom's boxes piled on the counter as they always were on Saturdays. She'd filled them with her winter produce, jams, breads, and hand-knit whatever-they-were. Her wares were ready to be taken for sale at the farmer's market, but thanks to me, she was late. She needed the pickup.

Voices came from somewhere in the house. I followed the noise to our sitting room, where Mom sat in front of a brand new flat-screen TV set on top of the case that held her ancient record collection. If this had happened two days ago, I probably would've fainted from shock, but now it seemed nothing could surprise me anymore. She hung on every word of the town infomercial like it was *The Holy Grail of Organic Farming* instead.

"Mom?"

She slowly turned to look at me.

"Where did you get this TV?"

"From Ike's Electronics."

"Why did you get this TV?"

"They gave it to us. Things are changing. We don't have to pay anymore. Isn't it wonderful?" She spoke in a complete monotone, like she'd memorized the words but her heart just wasn't in it.

Mom stood up. "I have to go to the market."

"Why?" Given the way she was right now, I wondered why she did anything at all.

"I have to do my job. All of us must do our jobs." She seemed to be parroting instructions she'd received.

"Did Captain Leach tell you that?" I couldn't think of anyone else who'd had the opportunity to order Mom around. Or anyone creepy enough to actually want to do it.

"Who?" she said, walking to the tap. She turned it on and water poured out.

"I... I thought the water had been cut," I said.

"The water main was shut off. I turned it back on." Mom filled a glass.

"Don't drink that, Mom."

She ignored me and brought the glass to her lips. I charged her and tore it from her hand, dumping out the water. She stared at me for a few seconds before turning and picking up one of her boxes. She carried it out to her truck.

What now? I couldn't stand here forever blocking her access to the tap. If I wasn't around, she would drink it. I considered locking her in a room for the next twenty-four hours until the drug cleared from her system. Unfortunately, it would have to be a closet to prevent her from escaping through a window. A small enclosed space like that would be stuffy, cramped, and uncomfortable, and she might hurt herself pounding on the door.

A better plan might be to bind her somehow, so she could lie on the bed and I would be able to keep an eye on her. Duct tape was the obvious choice but it might be painful to remove. Actual criminals probably never worried about that part. Whatever I decided, it would be best to approach her when she was sleeping so she wouldn't have a chance to struggle. I didn't want either of us getting hurt in a fight. The more I thought about it, the more I realized this was really a two or three-person job. I'd have to ask Randy and Giselle for their help.

In the meantime, I loaded the rest of Mom's boxes onto the truck. It was the least I could do after I'd made her late. I was pretty sure she snuck a quick glass of water while I was outside, but as I said, I couldn't watch her every second. When we were done, and she had driven away, I went upstairs to take a long, hot, luxurious shower, feeling like there was so much metaphorical grime to wash away. I kept my mouth clamped shut to be sure I didn't swallow a single drop and pushed away the disturbing thought that I might absorb the chemical's properties through my skin.

Our landline rang while I was getting dressed, and I dashed down the hall to the closest handset, which was on Mom's bedside table. I normally never answered because 99 percent of the time it was a robocall, or a scammer telling us we owed taxes to the IRS and that police were being dispatched to arrest us if we didn't buy them a fully loaded iTunes card.

When I reached the phone, I paused to check the display to see who was calling, like I would with my cell, until I realized this ancient machine didn't have a display. *Crap.* I went ahead and answered anyway, in case it might be Giselle or Randy.

Silence followed my greeting. I thought I heard light breathing, but it could've been my imagination. "Hello?" I repeated.

Still no response. I remembered now that long-distance calls weren't getting through. Probably the call had been cut off for that reason. I hung up and returned to my bedroom to finish dressing. Deciding it would be best to stick with practical clothing, I grabbed a fresh pair of jeans, a long-sleeved T, cotton socks and my Adidas. If I was going to have to wrestle with Mom later in the day, I better be dressed for it.

While I was tying my shoes, I started getting an uneasy feeling about that phone call. Maybe I was wrong, but it really had sounded like someone was on the line, breathing faintly. Also, if it had been a long-distance call, it probably wouldn't have rung. It never would've gotten through to us at all. My shoulders tensed on the sudden thought that the call might've been intended to find out if anyone was home.

I sprang up, ran to the window to look out at the driveway, and nearly had a heart attack to see a cop cruiser coasting down our hill. I couldn't hear a thing. They must've shut off the engine in order to sneak up on us.

I had to leave. *Fast.* I was certain if they caught me they would make me drink the water and then I would be exactly like Mom and there would be no hope for either of us. I had no time to formulate a plan before racing out the door to the back yard. My first thought was to dash toward the neighbor's house. But the cops would hear me and chances were good they'd be able to catch me too. I wasn't exactly Ms. Track Star, a fact I regretted as much as I'd bemoaned my lack of soccer skills the night before.

I heard the sound of a car door shutting, and then voices. "I'll check around back," one of them said.

No time remained to think. I took off down the hill toward the river.

"She's here!" the same officer shouted. Branches snapped as he pursued me.

Adrenalin whizzed through me and propelled me to the edge of the water. I hesitated at the thought of how freezing it would be this time of year.

"Police! Stop where you are!" That was a different voice; they were both coming after me now.

I couldn't wait any longer. I ran into the river and its icy grip stole my breath away. I forced myself onward until I was able to dive, submerging myself completely in the frigid, rushing water. It carried me away.

Chapter Seventeen

The current dragged me under, swirling me round and round until I couldn't tell which end was up. The glacial water wracked my body in agony. Breathless, I struggled to keep from thrashing in a panic, letting myself spin in the eddy for several seconds until it spat me out.

Now I could make out the surface from the brightness of the sun above. Pulling hard, I pushed my head above the water, gulping for air but choking on a mouthful of liquid instead. I swallowed more water as it slammed into my face. Flailing my arms and legs, I managed to lift my head again, and this time I sucked in a deep breath.

I turned myself so my feet were aimed downstream and would hit any rocks before my head did. There weren't any big drops coming up; I knew that much. At least not until Ragged Falls, a fifteen-foot plummet onto boulders. But I had a good twenty minutes before I would reach it. If I was still in the water then, I'd be dead of hypothermia anyway.

The river kept trying to drag me under, forcing me to work hard to stay afloat. I checked both sides. Downstream there was an empty field on the opposite bank from where we lived. I needed to cross over there, fighting the current that gripped me. Turning on my stomach to swim, I spied another whirlpool coming up fast. If I got ripped into it, no way would I reach the field when I popped out. *If* I popped out. Channeling Michael Phelps, I threw all my strength into my freestyle stroke. *Why didn't I join the swim team when Mom urged me?* For each foot

I moved across the river, I lost three being hauled downstream. It looked like I was going to miss the beach, and then it would be all over for me. From here on, high banks bound the river on both sides.

At the last possible moment, I lunged and caught hold of a low hanging branch from a tree growing at the edge of the water. I dragged myself along it, scraping my hands, until finally my feet touched bottom. It gave me the leverage I needed to hurl myself to shore. From there, I clawed my way forward until I reached dry sand, where I collapsed in an icy heap.

Probably five minutes passed before I managed to move again. I might've remained like that for hours and eventually died of exposure, but for my fear of the police. They would find me soon if I didn't get going.

Running also seemed like my only chance of warming up. My teeth were chattering, and my body shaking from head to toe as I forced myself to my feet. A path led along the river on this side, and though I knew it was risky to take it in case the cops chose the same route, I really didn't see any alternative. I began heading upstream at a slow jog—the only pace I could manage for the moment.

I needed to figure out my next move. Ben was the friend who lived closest to the river on this side. I could follow the trail for a mile, then switch to the road. Crossing the main street posed the biggest danger, but if I managed that, I'd probably be safe the rest of the way to his house. It was a quiet neighborhood that didn't lead anywhere; no one drove through unless they lived there.

Jogging was tough for me at the best of times, but with my jeans and tennis shoes completely soaked, it was a slog. I think the only thing that kept me going was the adrenaline still coursing through me. I reached Ben's house without incident, and found it closed up like before. I had been planning on knocking, but then I decided to just try the knob. The door was unlocked, and I opened it quietly. The drone of the infomercial came from the direction of the sitting room, sounding mostly the same though I thought they might've changed the script a bit.

Taking a couple steps, I froze at the squelching sound coming from my soaked shoes. I yanked them off and continued down the hallway, past the family room where Ben's mother and two brothers were seated around the blaring TV. Chances were good either Ben was upstairs, or he'd gone to the video game store, *Games, Games, and More Games*, where he worked part-time. As Mom had said, *all of us must do our jobs.*

I tiptoed past them and snuck to Ben's room on the second floor. Unsure how he'd react to my drenched appearance, I hoped he was out. My shoulders relaxed as I glanced through the open door into his empty room, ridiculously clean and organized as always, with the bots he'd designed for three years' worth of robotics competitions tucked into the corner, and space exploration posters hung neatly on the walls. Hilton's maid service could not have done a finer job making up the bed.

Going straight to his dresser, I got out a pair of plaid boxers from the impeccably folded stack in his top drawer. *My god, did he iron these things?* I found jeans in the next drawer, and a long-sleeved T in a plain color below that. In case he came home and wandered up here for some reason, I locked the door before stripping off all my wet things. Not seeing a towel, I dried my ass with his bedspread before putting on his clothes. The jeans were wide at the waist, but I stole a piece of rope from one of the bots and used it like a belt. Since Ben was taller than me, I also had to fold up the hem at the bottom.

I put on a thick sweatshirt I found in his closet. This was California and it often wasn't that cold in February, but I was still shivering from the dunking. I tried his shoes but they were way too big. Instead, I wore two thick pairs of his socks; they would have to do for now.

I stuffed my wet clothes and shoes in a black backpack I found hanging in his closet, since I would need them later when they dried off. Scanning the room for anything else that might be useful, my eyes stopped on his wallet, resting on his bedside table. For a minute I just stood there, staring at it, while I wrestled with my conscience. Borrowing clothes was one thing, but taking money felt like stealing.

In the end I left his wallet alone. Even if I couldn't go home for a while, Giselle would have money, and she'd gladly loan it to me. She gave money to anyone who asked. Even to some who didn't ask.

I crept out of Ben's room, down the stairs, and past the living room, where the family remained glued to the TV. Turning the corner toward the front door, I walked straight into Ben's dad.

"Sorry!" I said. "Nice to see you, Mr. Schwartz! I was looking for Ben. Is he at work?"

"No," he said, showing zero surprise at my being in his house. "He's at the hospital." He tried to move past me but I blocked him.

"What happened?" My first thought was the water must be killing him.

"He crashed the car coming home from work last night. He has a concussion. He'll be all right." Mr. Schwartz sidestepped me and headed to the family room to join his family in front of the TV.

I switched directions and went through the door into the garage. I couldn't allow myself to worry about Ben at the moment. First I had to get someplace safe. Ben would receive the care he needed in the hospital, if all the stupefied were driven like Mom to do their jobs.

One car was parked in the garage. Presumably the other had been taken to the shop following Ben's accident. I considered borrowing the car—the keys had been hanging from a hook in the kitchen—but they might eventually notice and even report it to the police. Since I couldn't leave town, the cops would find me easily, and then they'd actually have something to charge me with—felony grand theft.

Ben's bike was leaning against the right side of the garage. I put on his helmet and a pair of sunglasses I found. This would serve as a disguise as well as being good for safety. I pushed the button to open the garage door, praying no one inside would hear it, or if they did, would not be curious about it. I wheeled the bike out before the door was fully lifted, mounted it, and pedaled hard. I didn't worry too much about leaving the garage door open, since the family usually left it that way anyhow.

I rode as fast as I could toward Randy's place, terrified the cops might already have tracked down both my friends and forced them into joining the ranks of the stupefied.

Chapter Eighteen

When I buzzed Randy's apartment from the front of the building, his granny answered and told me he wasn't there. I heard the TV on in the background until she released the Intercom button. I tried to ask where he went, but that was the end of our conversation as far as she was concerned.

I pedaled to Giselle's next. Considering how much riding, running, and swimming I'd done today, pretty soon I'd be ready to join Randy's grandma at the triathlon, though no doubt she'd still beat me, given all her training. I cursed Giselle's steep driveway and ended up having to walk the bike up. When I got to the top, I went around to the side of the garage and peered in the window to see if Giselle's car was back. Unfortunately, it wasn't. It killed me not to be able to text her to find out where she and Randy were, and to warn them about the cops. I had no desire to end up as the last citizen of Los Patos who still had a working brain.

Retrieving the bike, I wheeled it to Giselle's entrance. I unlocked the door with her key and brought the bike inside, propping it below the window so no one peering in would see it. If the cops came, I didn't want them thinking anyone was here. Not to mention that the bike was stolen property. It would've helped if the windows had curtains, but I suppose Giselle's family thought that would block the view of the vineyards.

I sat on the couch, wondering if there was anything I could do at the moment. My eyelids grew heavy thinking about it, and I realized I needed to sleep after the ordeal I'd gone through. I got pillows and a blanket from Giselle's bedroom and set them on the floor behind the couch so I wouldn't be seen by prying eyes. My limbs felt the pull of gravity as I lay down and drew the cover over me. Sleep must've come right away.

The next thing I knew, the door to the outside was being rattled. My eyes jolted open and my first thought was to wish I'd brought some kind of weapon with me to my hideout behind the couch. But my second thought swatted the first one away. A trophy or a wine bottle wasn't going to cut it against the cops.

The next sound was that of Randy and Giselle laughing. *What could they possibly have to laugh about?* My blood heated at the idea that they might've gone somewhere and actually enjoyed themselves while I'd been busy worrying about them and, oh, trying to stay alive.

Their laughter cut off. "Is that yours?" Randy said. I figured he must be looking at the bike.

"It's Ben Schwartz's," I said, popping up from my hiding place.

Giselle let out a small screech and even Randy, who was low-key about everything, looked surprised.

"What're you doing?" Giselle said. "Why were you hiding?"

"I'm starving," I said. "I'll tell you over lunch." I glanced out the window at the darkening sky. "Dinner?"

We went up to the kitchen and Giselle let me pick a frozen veggie lasagna from the bottomless freezer. Feeling disgusted by water of any kind at the moment, I grabbed a Diet Coke from the fridge. I told them all about my terrible day while eating my microwaved meal and trying not to think about how Mom's veggie lasagna was a thousand times better than this one.

"You shouldn't have gone home," Randy said.

"Um, I seem to remember someone ignoring that same advice last night." I shoved in my last bit of cardboard lasagna and washed it down with the metallic Coke, beginning to think Mom had ruined me for junk food.

Giselle interrupted to prevent an argument. "We went to Jamie's Café for a late lunch. Sat there for a while just watching people. Sierra, there's no chatting anymore. Everyone's just, like, doing a job. Eating their meal and leaving. Or the workers, same thing. Take the order, make the sandwich, collect the money. Then just stand there silently till another customer orders something."

"Like they're all hypnotized," Randy added.

"Stupefied." I glanced at movement out the front windows, but it was just branches swaying in the wind. "I don't think we're safe here. The cops could find out who my friends are. We need someplace to hide."

They were silent while I chowed down a few Oreos from the pack Giselle had gotten out.

She cast an uneasy glance toward the driveway. "I know where we can hide... the wine cellar. If the police come here, I doubt they'll bother to search the whole property. They'll just figure we went to some other kid's house."

Randy shrugged. "Might as well."

I felt like he was avoiding looking at me. It was definitely awkward being the third wheel in this little ménage à trois, but the problem was much bigger than any high school relationship drama. Giselle's idea was solid, and I told her so.

We could always move from the wine cellar if we thought of something better later on. But how much effort would police devote to the search for three high school students? Very little, I thought. Whatever diabolical plan had been put into place here in Los Patos, it was crazy to believe we could make a dent in it.

71

The wine cellar was built into the side of the hill to help insulate the wine from ever getting too hot, according to Giselle. It had a cement floor and a high wooden ceiling to accommodate the tall stacks of wine barrels. The front part of the cellar had an open area where they'd put a wooden picnic table with benches, for when guests were invited to taste wine directly from the barrels. The only space aside from that consisted of walkways in between the stacks.

After moving the picnic table next to the wall to make more room for our bedding, we spent the next three hours bringing supplies from the house. In the end we had sleeping bags, blow-up mattresses, and cooking supplies, along with boxes of food, sodas, juices and water bottles. And winter jackets. The cellar was kept at a frigid temperature because it was designed for preserving wine, not people. Giselle was adamant that we couldn't turn the thermostat up. Despite our local apocalypse—or whatever this was—she would not risk ruining her parents' entire inventory of premium wine.

The cellar had no windows and even with the lights on, it was a dim and shadowy place soaked in the aroma of red wine. The scent was so powerful I thought we could get drunk on it. But maybe a little buzz would take our minds off our troubles.

When we were finally settled in, we sat down to eat another small meal and formulate our next steps. I had an idea for what we ought to do. Unfortunately, we would need to do it tonight.

Chapter Nineteen

I rang the doorbell three times before Myles came. That was the same number of times it had taken Ben to answer the first day, before his accident. It seemed like obsessive-compulsive disorder was part of the package. Everything had to be repeated three times. Or maybe they were just slow to react.

Myles was chewing when he opened the door and had the glazed look I was coming to expect from everyone. The smell of charred steak hit my nose and got my stomach juices churning, even though I'm a vegetarian. I peered past Myles into the house and glimpsed his two dads at the dinner table. Not talking, just mechanically putting bites of meat into their mouths. One of them, Mr. Kaneko—who preferred if Myles' friends called him Denji—glanced my way and stared for a second or two before turning back to his meal. It was creepy, but I didn't think he meant anything threatening. The stupefied just did everything slower than normal folk.

"Hey," I said to Myles. "I'm headed to Oh-Yum's for ice cream sandwiches. Want to come?" They were made by hand and tasted like bliss.

Myles actually appeared to think about it, until he said, "No, thanks," and tried to shut the door. Acting quickly, I thrust my foot in the way, nearly getting it crushed.

"Ow!" I said. I pushed the door back into Myles and inserted myself in the opening. His refusal to take the ice cream bait meant I needed to move into phase two. I "accidentally" brushed a breast of mine against his bicep and murmured, "I missed you at the party last night." I touched his cheek and whispered, "Let's go to my place. Mom isn't home."

I tried not to take it personally when he refused me faster than he'd rejected the ice cream treat. *He has no idea what he's giving up*, I told myself. Or maybe I just sucked at being a femme fatale.

"I have to finish dinner now," he said. "It's important to have balanced meals."

"Whatevs," I said, backing up and pretending to fall down his front door steps. This was phase three of the plan and I didn't do it very well. "Ow!" I cried out louder than before because I landed badly on my back. Although the pain was on my rear side, I grabbed my ankle dramatically like Mom had done the day before. "I think I sprained it!"

Myles paused, watching me.

"Help me up," I said. "Please?" I did my best damsel-in-distress act.

He had to think about it, but at last he came out of the house and bent down to give me a hand.

Randy jumped out from the side, came up behind Myles, and poked him in the back with something in his pocket. "It's a gun," he said in a threatening voice. "Do what we say and you won't get hurt." I got the impression he was kind of enjoying himself.

Of course, it wasn't a gun, it was the bottom end of Giselle's electric toothbrush.

But the stupefied still had some sense of self-preservation, because Myles straightened up and said, "Okay."

Giselle, driving her parents' Tesla, zipped to the curb from where she had been waiting down the street and stopped sharp like this was a bank holdup getaway. "Get in," she said through the lowered passenger window.

Randy pushed Myles into the back seat while I got in the front. Giselle stomped on the pedal, throwing us all backwards in our seats as the car shot forward. I looked back to see Mr. Kaneko at the door, staring at our car with a confused expression. He didn't look worried, though. He'd seen me, so he probably figured Myles had gone to hang out with friends. With luck he'd simply return to his meal and forget all about it.

"Slow down!" I shouted at Giselle. It was early enough in the evening that other cars were on the road, probably people returning from their jobs or the grocery store. But a Tesla careening down the road was still going to attract attention.

She threw me an annoyed look but did as I asked. We both knew her speeding had everything to do with the Tesla being such a cool car to drive, and nothing to do with our needing to get away fast from his stupefied parents, who could care less.

We made it back to Giselle's house without incident. Randy and I walked Myles to the wine cellar while Giselle put the car back in the garage. Randy ordered Myles to lie down on his side on top of the open sleeping bag while I wrapped duct tape around his wrists behind his back, and then did the same to his ankles. Randy and I had argued about whether we should do his wrists in front or back, with me arguing for the front because it wouldn't be so uncomfortable. Giselle was on my side, but eventually Randy convinced me Myles might manage to escape if he had his hands in front of him. And the whole point of doing this was to save Myles, so it wouldn't help him if we were sloppy or incomplete in the job. But now, here I was having to tape him and hating myself for doing it. At least he didn't struggle, but he looked so pathetic I felt terrible for him. Worst of all, I was certain if he remembered this he'd never forgive me.

When we were done, he didn't even ask us why we kidnapped him. He just looked up with empty eyes and asked for a glass of water. I held out a Diet Coke instead, but he shook his head. "Water," he repeated.

"I'm sorry, no," I said. Giselle and Randy and I had already speculated that the water might be addictive along with everything else. That was main reason we wanted Myles right here in the room with us, so we could keep an eye out for withdrawal symptoms.

Giselle joined us and sat down. "And now we wait," she said.

That was the plan. It hadn't been easy to convince Randy and Giselle to go along with this kidnapping idea. A lot of things could've gone wrong, like our getting caught by the cops and forced to drink the water. But I argued that if we were going to fight this thing... if we had any hope of finding out what was happening to everyone we cared for... we needed reinforcements. I picked Myles because, well, I liked him. Hey, Giselle had Randy. But he was against picking Myles, because he didn't like him. I insisted Myles would be an asset due to his being an athlete: the star player on the boys' soccer team. That didn't impress Randy in the slightest. But when Giselle took my side, he gave up arguing.

Myles was our test case. We would prevent him from drinking the tap water and see if the effects began to wear off. We had no clue how long this might take, or if it would work at all, or if it might hurt him. This uncertainty was the main reason I hadn't suggested my mother as our first subject. She could be the second if all went well. Although we didn't have a plan yet for fixing our town, at least, if it turned out to be possible to cure the stupefied, it would give us some hope.

While Myles lay there staring at the wall, we played three rounds of The Settlers of Catan. I won two but had to concede the third to Randy. I'm very competitive when it comes to games, whereas Giselle could care less. My strong desire to crush my opponents distracted me from my anxiety over Myles' situation, and from wondering every minute if he was starting to get better.

When it was time to sleep, we decided we should take turns so that one person would always be awake. That was because Myles could possibly get up and hop to the door if he really tried hard. Plus we needed to keep a lookout for cops.

Giselle kept the first watch while Randy and I slept. She woke me after three hours. "All's quiet," she said before lying down on her mat and falling instantly asleep.

I dragged myself out of my sleeping bag and cracked open another can of caffeine-laden soda. I was groggy, feeling like I needed about ten more hours of sleep, I guess because of my ordeal earlier in the day. A glance at Myles told me he was sleeping despite the discomfort of being duct-taped. I went and sat near the door since there weren't any windows, and I thought that position might give me a better chance of hearing cop cars approaching outside. The cellar had a back way out if we needed to use it.

After sitting for ten minutes, I got bored and decided to take a walk outside. The fresh air would help clear my head and finish the job of waking me up. Plus I realized I couldn't hear anything through the thick wine cellar door, so it wouldn't hurt to glance around the property.

I opened the door as quietly as I could, closing it after me. I drew in a deep breath of the crisp air and strolled over toward the tasting room. As I rounded the corner and looked up the driveway toward the house, I glimpsed red brake lights through the trees.

My breath caught in my throat. I couldn't make out the car, but it had to be cops. Turning, I sprinted back to the wine cellar, yanking the door open and shutting it hard behind me.

Randy's eyes shot open.

"Police!" I said.

Myles screamed.

Chapter Twenty

Randy threw himself on top of Myles, clapping his hand over Myles' mouth. "Duct tape!" he shouted at me, while he tried to muffle the screams.

My heart was racing. *Duct tape.* My head snapped to where I thought we'd left it.

"Shit!" Randy cried out.

I turned back to find Randy staring down at his bloody hand where Myles had bitten him. Myles began screaming again, which prompted Randy to hold Myles' head on top and under the chin, forcing his jaw shut. At the same time, Myles was kicking and kneeing Randy, and it was all Randy could do to stay on top of him.

I continued my frantic search for the duct tape and scissors, finally locating them on the table behind some boxes. I cut off a piece as fast as I could, while Randy struggled to keep his hand out of Myles' biting range.

"Here!" I said, rushing over.

"Put it on him!" Randy said.

I bent down and slapped on the tape while Randy tried to hold him steady, nearly getting bitten myself in the process. Randy and I both leapt backwards out of reach of the flailing Myles.

The tape held. Myles thrashed his head from side to side like a tortured animal, making noises in his throat, but the screaming stopped.

Randy looked at me. "You had to say that out loud?"

"You mean, 'police'?" I said. "I thought he was asleep!"

"He probably was until you shouted." Randy bent over Giselle and started shaking her. Astonishingly, she'd slept through all the noise.

"Well you're welcome for warning you!" It seemed like nothing I ever did was right, according to Randy.

"We gotta go," he told Giselle when she finally opened her eyes.

"They might not have heard us," I said. "The door is thick."

"If you want to stay and find out, feel free," he said.

Giselle was sitting up, staring at us groggily. He helped her to her feet.

"They might see us outside. We could be safer just staying here." I looked at Giselle for agreement, but she was still too dazed to offer an opinion.

Randy drew Giselle toward the rear exit. He paused and turned back. "*C'mon*," he whispered.

I felt smug thinking despite what he said before, it bothered him to leave me behind.

"What about Myles?" I said.

"If they find him, he'll be no worse off than he already is."

I was torn leaving Myles by himself, but Randy was right. Plus it seemed smarter to keep together as a team, and Randy's muscles were a lot bigger than mine. I hurried toward them.

Randy cracked the door and peered out. We were facing the downward slope of the vineyard, with the house and driveway on the other side. Randy put his finger to his lips.

Like I didn't already know to be quiet, I thought.

We tiptoed out and I shut the door behind us. Shaking off her drowsiness, Giselle took the lead since she knew the family vineyards best. Randy and I followed in the darkness, past gnarly, leafless vines that bordered us on both sides like ancient hands reaching out from the grave. But the plants provided no cover in February, and my stomach clenched at the thought that searching eyes could easily spot us, despite the lack of a moon in the sky.

Giselle led us to a grove of pine trees, and we hid ourselves where we could glimpse the road. She pressed against Randy for warmth and he put his arm around her. When I glanced their way, he avoided my eyes.

A few minutes later, we saw the car turn onto the road from the bottom of the driveway.

"It's not a cop car," Randy whispered, throwing an accusing look at me.

"I couldn't tell," I hissed back. "It might've been. Anyway, who's going to come here at this hour? Must've been them in an unmarked."

The vehicle drove away at a normal speed, not looking in a hurry to get anywhere.

We went back to the wine cellar.

***

Myles had calmed down by the time we returned, and just lay there as before with his eyes closed. He might've fallen back to sleep, or he might've been faking it. Either way I didn't want to disturb him. Most likely even if he returned to normal, he wouldn't ever want to talk to me again after the way I'd taped him up.

Randy said he didn't think he could sleep anymore and volunteered to take over the watch. I got in my sleeping bag while Giselle put antiseptic on his bite wound and bandaged it. When they started laughing and whispering among themselves, I pulled the bag up over my head and turned the other way, wishing I could sleep like the dead the way Giselle did. I guess I did dose off, but mainly it was a restless sleep, filled with disturbing dreams that I fortunately couldn't remember when I woke up.

Randy was at the table eating a bowl of cereal when I rose and glanced around. "Where's Giselle?" I asked.

"Getting blankets at the house." He nodded toward Myles.

I approached Myles, who now lay on his other side. Randy must've shifted him, which was thoughtful. Myles looked awful, though. His skin was pale and his face and forehead were beaded with sweat. He was trembling all over. No doubt being in here was like living in a refrigerator, but this was something more.

Randy came over and stood beside me.

"Looks like fever chills," I said.

"I think it's withdrawal," Randy said.

"We should give him some water."

Randy nodded, and I fetched a bottle from our supplies. He lifted Myles into a sitting position, while I kneeled beside him.

"Myles," I said, making eye contact with him. "There's no one outside to hear you scream. It won't help to bite anyone either. You understand?"

He looked at me blankly and then slowly nodded.

"We don't want to hurt you. We're trying to cure you. You've been poisoned by the tap water," I said. "We have to keep you like this until the poison is gone from your system. Now, do you want some of this?" I held up the bottle.

He nodded his head vigorously.

"Great. I'm going to take the duct tape off your mouth, and then you can drink." I picked at an edge of the tape and pulled it. Myles made a sound in his throat which I was sure would've been "Ow!" and then I stopped.

Randy got impatient, grabbed the other edge, and yanked the whole thing off at once.

"Yow!" Myles cried out.

81

I was relieved to see he still had all his skin, and though I would never admit it, I was grateful to Randy. Thanks to him, I had at least not been responsible for this latest atrocity against Myles. I opened the bottle and put it to Myles' lips while he tipped his head back and sucked it down. Maybe a third of the water ended up in his lap, but it was the best I could manage.

The door opened and Giselle entered with an armful of blankets.

"You want more water?" I said to Myles. He shook his head in response. "Something to eat?" I added. He shook his head again. Randy helped him lie back down.

"We should cover his mouth again," Randy said quietly to me.

"I don't think we need to," I said.

Randy looked like he wanted to argue some more.

"I agree with Sierra," Giselle said, laying a blanket over Myles.

Randy turned away.

***

We played cards and board games most of the afternoon and evening, taking time out for eating. I was worried about Myles and wondered if we should bring him to a doctor, but at the same time I realized that would put us all in jeopardy. I checked on him frequently and he seemed about the same. He drifted off to sleep now and then, but it didn't look like a restful sleep the way he was tossing and turning.

After dinner we decided to sit down with pen and paper and make a list of the things we could do to try to get to the bottom of what was happening in our town. We had just written: "Go to Verizon store and demand to know what happened to our service," when all of a sudden we heard Myles' voice behind us.

"Sierra," he said. "What the hell's going on?"

Chapter Twenty-One

Myles was restored. We cut off his bindings and spent the next hour filling him in on everything that had happened since he became one of the stupefied. He sat at the table and ate a bologna sandwich, a PB&J, and an entire box of Cheez-its, washing it all down with orange soda.

"What about you?" I said after we'd finished explaining. "What do you remember about the last two days? Not much, right?" I was desperately hoping the answer was *nothing* so we wouldn't have to talk about the duct tape.

"I remember everything," he said. "But it was like there was a fog in my head. Know what I mean? Nothing interested me. I only felt like drinking a lot of water and watching TV."

"Dude, what is it with the TV?" Randy said. "Why is everyone watching it?"

"It kind of felt... soothing. Hypnotizing, I guess."

The three of us exchanged a look. "That's how it looks," I said.

"While I was watching, I kept thinking, relax... don't ask questions... keep to yourself... just do your job."

"What job?" Giselle said.

"Homework. I got two projects done that aren't due for a week."

That wasn't the slightest bit normal for Myles, who usually completed homework assignments an hour before they were due.

"Who's doing this to us?" he said. "And why?"

Now it was our turn to look blank-faced.

"We should get the hell out of here," Randy said, breaking the silence.

"We tried that, remember?" said Giselle.

I knew what he meant because I'd thought about it too. "Since the roads are blocked, we'll have to walk out," I said.

"The Starke Lake trail goes to Wilder. It's not that many miles," Randy said.

"I'm not ready to go," Myles said.

We all looked at him.

"What if Wilder's just as bad as Los Patos? What if we leave and then can't get back here to our families?"

"We won't know until—"

"Just saying there's a lot we don't know," Myles said. "Maybe, before running away, we should try to find out more."

"How?" Giselle looked at him sincerely. She really wanted to know.

"I'm going to school tomorrow. Maybe there are still some people who aren't affected. I need to see for myself," Myles said. "And then I want to check on my dads."

"Me too," I added quietly. "I mean, I want to go to school and check on Mom. See if we can find any other normal people. If not... we can leave town tomorrow night. We should go when it's dark anyway."

Giselle rubbed my arm. "The police are looking for you, Sierra."

"They probably figured I drowned," I said. "Besides, how much effort are they going to put into tracking down a high school kid?"

"Let's do it then," Giselle said. "Just for tomorrow, and then we leave."

Randy got up without saying anything. I could tell from his expression that he didn't like it, but since he didn't protest, it looked like we would all be headed back to school in the morning.

***

We rose early, shoved down some breakfast, and set out. Giselle had wanted to drive us in the Tesla, as she desperately hoped to get some advantage out of her parents being unable to return home. But we all knew that would attract attention. Of course the stupefied wouldn't notice it, but I wasn't sure how many in the police force were stupefied. The chief certainly didn't seem to be. And being a geek, he would definitely notice a Tesla.

Instead, Randy left on his skateboard, I took Ben's bike, Giselle had her own bike, and Myles used Giselle's dad's bike. We took different routes to school. Better if one or two of us were caught, but not all.

Unlike on Friday, I made it on time to my first period calculus class and settled into a seat in the back so I could watch everyone. It was a "normal" lesson if you lived in *every-kid-does-exactly-what-adults-tell-them-to-do* town. All the students paid rapt attention to the problems Mrs. Suarez wrote on the board. No one talked, checked their text messages, or fell asleep.

Everyone in class was stupefied, in other words. I had expected as much, but a small part of me had deeply hoped I was wrong. Seeing the reality, it was hard not to feel discouraged. I wondered if there was any point in going to my other classes. When the time was nearly up, I packed my backpack and prepared to move on to my next period because that's what my friends and I had agreed we would do, not because I had any expectation of discovering another unaffected person.

The bell rang and I got up, thinking the students would race out of the class as they normally did, but of course, being stupefied, they instead waited submissively at their desks for Mrs. Suarez to dismiss them. Before she could do that, the door opened and a visitor walked in.

My chin hit the floor.

The visitor dropped off a folder for Mrs. Suarez, then paused to look at everyone in the classroom before heading back out.

Mrs. Suarez said, "Thank you, Mr. Meena," which was our principal's name. But it wasn't Mr. Meena.

He, or rather *it*, was an artificial being made up to look roughly like Mr. Meena, including his thick, black curly hair and his goofy mode of dress. But the visitor, with its smooth plastic skin, resembled a mannequin far more than a human being. Its most unsettling feature was its black eyes, which had rapidly shifted their focus around the room, staring at each of us in perfectly timed intervals, as no person ever could've done. Like a timer had been going off in its head... *click*, Jason... *click*, Hannah... *click*, Sierra. During the fraction of a second when its eyes connected with mine, the hair lifted on my arms.

No one in their right mind could mistake this android for a man. But sadly, the students and teachers of Los Patos High School were not in their right minds.

Chapter Twenty-Two

After the shock of seeing Principal Droid, I'm not sure how I managed to stand up and get out of the classroom. I felt sick to my stomach and had to pause by the door, leaning against the wall, watching my brain-dead classmates filing out to the corridor. An unnatural stillness replaced the usual chaos that broke out between periods, with students forming into neat lanes to march robotically to their next classes.

I broke through their ranks to cross the hall to the girl's bathroom, pushing in the door, stumbling against the nearest stall. I didn't go in, just lay my head against the metal as tears of frustration filled my eyes.

Am I losing my mind? was all I could think. Maybe I was the stupefied one… I was having hallucinations… I'd lost my grip on reality. I was trapped inside a horrifying, unending nightmare. *Can I trust my own eyes anymore?* The more I thought about it, the more it seemed I must've imagined everything. It was the only explanation that made sense… the only one that accounted for all the craziness, from tainted water and Skeleton Man, to Robot Mr. Meena. Far more likely that one person—me—had gone insane, rather than an entire town full of people. I wondered if I was already living in an asylum, and if the tap water represented the medicine my fucked-up mind refused to take.

I squeezed my eyes shut but couldn't hold back the tears pushing through and rolling down my cheeks. I clapped my hands over my ears. If I shut the world out, would I become sane again? Maybe if I didn't turn around, didn't look at anything, didn't listen to the sounds of their shuffling steps, the lunacy would go away and all would return to normal.

A hand touched my back and I screamed. *Oh my god it's the android.* There was nowhere to run so I ducked my head and clenched my arms around myself, closing up like a turtle. *Don't make me look at that thing,* was all I could think.

"Sierra." Randy's voice came through like a lifeline to the drowning. "I saw you come in here." He breathed in heavily. "I passed it walking down the hall. I knocked over two other guys jumping out of its path."

A few more seconds went by before his words penetrated my consciousness. *I passed it walking down the hall.* He meant the android. I wasn't crazy. He'd seen it too.

I turned around and through my tears I glimpsed his eyes, as lost and frightened as mine must have appeared. He put his arms around me and I wet his shoulder with more crying. I didn't feel guilty toward Giselle because there wasn't anything sexual about our contact. We were two people floundering in an ocean of madness, comforting each other the only way we knew how.

Randy might have been as scared as I was, but his strong presence soothed me. Eventually my tears dried up and I pulled away to fetch toilet paper from the stall. I wiped my face and blew my nose, feeling a flash of guilt for having snotted up Randy's T-shirt. I grabbed a paper towel and blotted the spot for him. He actually smiled a bit at that.

"We're so screwed," he said.

"Is it all connected?" I said. "I guess it must be."

"It's like a bad joke."

"It must be Pardize, right? Where else could that thing have come from? They're making androids to replace us."

"They're doing a shitty job of it," Randy said. "You can't mistake that thing for a person."

88

"I guess that's why they have to drug everyone," I said.

"They gonna drug the whole world?"

We stared at each other. It was one of the many, many questions I had. How far out from Los Patos did the craziness extend?

Randy moved toward the door. "We need to grab the others and get the hell out of here."

I nodded. I didn't want to spend one more minute than necessary in the same building with Robot Mr. Meena.

"Okay," he said. "You get Myles, I'll get Giselle. We make up some shit to get them out of class. Meet at the bikes."

"Right." I went to the sink, rinsed my face in water, and dried it with a paper towel. I thought it might be better not to freak my friends out with the signs of my recent meltdown all over my face. They might not have seen the android yet and we would need time to break that news to them. *Mr. Meena isn't the man he used to be* was a possible beginning.

Randy led the way out of the bathroom. The hallway was deadly silent as all the students had gone into their classrooms. I was about to turn and ask if he knew Giselle's schedule when we heard a voice coming from the other end of the hall.

"Stop right there." It sounded like Mr. Meena's baritone, complete with his Indian accent, except this voice held an undertone of menace.

Randy and I froze in place and exchanged a sideways glance. I believe Randy's meant, *should we run?*

I gave a subtle shake of the head, though I was quaking in my shoes.

Principal Droid walked around to face us. His gaze was penetrating, particularly since long intervals passed between his blinks. A scream formed in my throat. I swallowed hard to suppress it and stared down at my feet so I wouldn't have to look at him, wondering whether Randy was doing the same.

"Why aren't you in your classrooms?" the droid said.

That this mechanical man was acting like an actual principal concerned about our classroom attendance came across as a surreal nightmare. I opened my mouth but words would not come out.

"Follow me," he said.

We didn't dare refuse. I stared at the back of the droid in mingled fear and fascination as it took measured steps down the hallway, each one precisely like the other.

We continued in silence till we were outside Madame Moreau's French class. Robot Mr. Meena looked at Randy. Randy looked at me.

"See you later," I said in a strangled voice that didn't sound like my own.

Randy disappeared into the room.

The droid then led me to my second period class, American Lit. I wasn't surprised at its ability to identify Randy and me without asking. It must've used facial recognition software to find us in its database and retrieve our schedules. Although I understood the process, the thought of this machine having full access to everything the school knew about me made my skin crawl.

I was never so relieved to enter my American Lit class and shut the door behind me, but fear of Principal Droid waiting to escort me again when I came out kept my palms clammy and stomach tight for the rest of the period.

Chapter Twenty-Three

One thing was certain, I wasn't going to skip any more periods today. But at least creepy Robot Mr. Meena wasn't waiting for me outside American Lit when it was over. I went directly to US History and sat beside Giselle in the back. She whispered to me that she hadn't found anyone normal in her classes. I had to break the news about the droid to her, though I think she failed to grasp the full horror without actually seeing it.

We sat through the boring class counting the seconds till it was over. After I told her Principal Droid was keeping tabs on students, Giselle agreed we should finish out the school day even though it looked like we had no chance of encountering an un-stupefied person. We separated when the bell rang, with her intending to meet Randy for lunch, and me setting off in search of Myles.

He wasn't at any of the outside tables where I would usually find him on a sunny day like this one. I checked the indoor eating area without spotting him. Finally it occurred to me he might be at the soccer field, where he often liked to get in a quick scrimmage during the lunch break. I guess I hadn't thought of it sooner because I couldn't picture him finding anyone to play with him.

I was right about that, but it hadn't stopped him from practicing by himself. Approaching the bleachers, I watched Myles blast a ball at the goal. He had a mountain of balls next to him, and just kept slamming one after the other. I'd never seen him kick so many power balls in a row. He radiated a manic energy that both attracted and repelled me.

When I reached the field, I called out to him, and he sent off the last two balls before running to join me at the sidelines. I thought at once that he must have seen Robot Mr. Meena, given the fierce expression of his eyes and the way he held his arms stiff at his sides, with his hands balled into fists.

"I'm fucked," he said.

"We're all fucked."

"No, you don't get it. This quarantine. We can't play other towns. There's no soccer team anymore."

"That's what you're worried about?" It was difficult to keep the incredulity out of my voice. Clearly he had not run into Principal Droid.

He detected my tone and nearly kicked the bleachers. "Did you know Stanford was scouting me? Stanford! They're number three in the US."

I thought it best not to say that if we were taken over by robots, it might mean the end of the university system.

"Do you know how hard I've worked to get here? The millions of hours of practice since I was four years old… the dedication it's taken to play in three different soccer leagues plus my school team? Killing myself to reach the level where I'd be scouted by the best colleges?"

I scraped my shoe against the gravel.

His shoulders slumped. "I know I should be worried about the bigger picture. But my father—Denji—I can't disappoint him."

"It's like, he won't even be proud of me if I don't go to a top ten university," he said. "I've tried, but… I can't get the grades… you know how bad I am at math. So I thought, hey, why not soccer? I'll get in that way."

"I'm sorry," I said, meaning *I regret seeing you so unhappy*. Mr. Kaneko was wrong to push his own ambitions on his son like that.

"The game today was a big deal. Stanford's not going to wait around for me. They'll scout someone else." Myles threw himself down on the bleachers and hung his head.

I sat beside him. Neither one of us spoke for several minutes.

"You're not the only one with dreams," I said at last. "I've worked my ass off too... studied like crazy for the math SATs. I want to go someplace great and major in math or physics. I could see myself doing research in physics eventually."

I breathed out heavily. "It's too soon for us to give up hope. Any minute, help might arrive. The FBI, the National Guard... I don't know. There's got to be someone out there wondering what's happening in Los Patos."

"Unless it's happening everywhere..." Myles said.

I hugged myself to stifle a tremor inside. Myles laid his arm over my shoulder. "Sorry," he said. "Didn't mean to take it out on you."

My heart stretched out to him then. "I don't blame you. I'm pissed off too."

The bell rang, signaling the end of lunch period. "We have to go back," I said. "Mr. Meena is a droid and he'll find us."

It was a measure of the depth of Myles" misery that he barely registered my news at all.

Chapter Twenty-Four

Chem was my last class of the day and I was anxious to be done with it. Ben, my friend whose bike I'd stolen, was the only student absent from class. This worried me. Last I spoke to his father, Ben had been in the hospital after getting a concussion in a car accident. He must still be in pretty bad shape not to have come to school. The idea of doing your "job" seemed pretty ingrained in the stupefied. Claire was in class even though from her pale, clammy face, it looked as if she had a fever. Plus her nose was running and she couldn't stop coughing. But still she'd shown up to do her job, despite that she was normally the sort to use a hangnail as an excuse to skip school for the day.

Our chemistry teacher was named Mr. Black, which somehow always made me think of Mr. White from *Breaking Bad*. Maybe because unlike Mr. White, I could easily picture Mr. Black as a master criminal right from the start. He had a snarling voice and a quick temper whenever anyone made a mistake, which was all the time. Today, however, for the first time, experiments were proceeding smoothly because the students actually paid attention to the explanation before starting.

I was thinking about Ben while my lab partner, Heather, did the work. Usually it was the other way around, so I felt no guilt about putting it all on her. At one point she said something I didn't hear, which drew my attention back to the present. I stared at the kit she was using, and how the solution was packed in a plastic bag, and the image of a hospital IV bag flashed into my head. I wasn't sure, but it occurred to me they were probably sent to hospitals like that, already prepared and filled with solution, rather than, say, some orderly mixing up the magic potion and pouring it into a bag for each patient. And if that was the case… if the bags were prepared a while back, in some factory in some other city, then it was likely the water wasn't tainted.

Which meant that if Ben had been getting his fluids from an IV bag for the past couple of days, he might now be un-stupefied.

We needed Ben. He was the best person I knew to deal with computer hardware. He'd won the robotics competition two years in a row, and if we ever needed a robotics expert, it was now. I liked to believe I was as good with software, but when it came to tinkering with machines, he was the best. Also, thanks to his dad being a handyman, Ben had a basic understanding of everything practical: electronics, woodworking, even plumbing. I couldn't think of a more useful person for our team. Not to mention he was my friend and I wanted to help him.

After chemistry let out, I raced to the bike racks in the parking lot to meet up with my friends. All of them were there before me, and from the morose looks on their faces, I didn't expect to hear any good news.

"We think we should leave Los Patos and find help," Myles said.

Randy and Giselle nodded in agreement.

"I saw the android." Giselle hugged herself, suppressing a shiver.

"Tonight," Randy said. "After dark. The Starke Lake trail."

"Count me in," I said. The thought of getting out of Los Patos gave me a glimmer of hope. I pictured rescue awaiting us only a few miles away. The fact that so much effort had been made to keep the town isolated made it more likely life was still normal outside our borders.

"There's one thing I need to do this afternoon," I said. "Ben Schwartz needs our help."

"Why him?" Myles said.

95

"He's in the hospital with a concussion. He must've been getting IV drips, which means he could've been cured of the water by now."

"Maybe," said Myles.

"At least we should go there and see how he is," Giselle said.

I could always count on her to vote for the kindest option. "We need to drive to the hospital," I said. "In case Ben isn't walking too well."

"We can use my granny's car," Randy said.

Giselle looked at me. "I just remembered something."

"What is it?" I said.

"It might not be safe to go to the hospital. You know, the plague?"

"They just made that up."

"Maybe. But what if they didn't?"

Everyone was silent for a moment, considering. "I'm willing to take the chance," Randy said.

"Me too," I said.

"Okay," said Giselle.

"I need to go home," Myles said. "I have to check in with my parents. They might be worried about me."

It was reasonable to want to see his dads, but I was a little disappointed. I had been hoping Myles would contribute more to our efforts. Today I was seeing a whole new side to him. In the past, he'd always been nice outside of his own group of jock and cheerleader types. In fact, I admired his ability to move easily between all the different cliques. But navigating high school melodrama was one thing and facing a water zombie robot apocalypse something else entirely. I guess it took the latter to really get to know someone.

I made a mental note to check in on Mom before the end of the day too, but it would have to wait till we rescued Ben, if that was even possible.

"Meet us back at Giselle's by sunset," I told Myles. I almost said "sundown," because if I was going to play the part of a western outlaw I might as well talk like one, but I was afraid my friends would just laugh at me.

"Sure," Myles said, hopping on his bike and taking off toward the street.

I glanced back at the school. Principal Droid stood on the front steps with his head turned toward us. I was certain he must have telescopic vision and could see us as clearly as if we stood directly in front of him. A cold spasm shot through my spine at the thought that he might have extremely good hearing as well. Or the ability to read lips.

"Let's get out of here," I said.

Chapter Twenty-Five

We agreed before going to the hospital we would all pretend to be stupefied at the reception desk. This meant showing no interest in the people around us, adopting a facial tic, and speaking in a monotone. The problem was, watching Randy squeeze his eyes shut, and Giselle jerk her face sideways just made me want to laugh. We decided maybe the tics weren't necessary since not all of those affected seemed to have them.

We began by strolling past the front desk as if we didn't even see it, hoping the woman seated there wouldn't notice us. Once again, we underestimated the urge these people felt to perform their jobs exactly as required. A security guard standing by the wall moved to block our way and ushered us back toward check-in. I stepped ahead of Randy and Giselle to speak to the woman, who looked to be about my mother's age and was so tiny her head barely rose above the level of the counter. A strong fragrance of lavender surrounded her, presumably her perfume or maybe just a scent she sprayed to combat the hospital odors.

"We're here to see Ben Schwartz," I said, noticing the woman's coffee mug was filled with water.

"Are you family?" she said.

"Yes," I lied.

She typed on her keyboard, stared at the screen, and looked back at us. "You aren't family. He has parents and two younger brothers."

"We're like family. That's what I meant. We're like the sisters and older brother he never had."

"I can't let you through."

"How about just me?"

"No, my orders are family only." It made her sound like a member of the Gestapo.

I glanced down the hall and saw a sign for the ladies' room. "I have to go to the bathroom. Very, very badly. May I use that one?" I hopped back and forth a bit to show how urgent it was.

"You may use the bathroom but you must return here when you're done," she said.

"Of course, I always do what I'm told," I said, trying to act more stupefied. I threw a look at Randy and Giselle as I went past them. Randy sauntered into position between the woman at the desk and her view of the restroom door. Giselle did the same with the security guard. I went into the bathroom, waited a few seconds, then peered back out.

Randy and Giselle were doing their best to block their prospective targets. Giselle moved to the guard's other side, drawing his eyes to her ass as she pretended to drop something and pick it up. At least there were some instincts that stupefication couldn't quite erase, though sadly my own lame attempt at seduction had fallen flat. I took advantage of the gatekeepers' distraction to slip out of the bathroom and continue around the corner to the elevator. Though I could not be seen by the welcome desk and the hall was empty, jitters ran through me as I pressed the button and waited. When the elevator arrived and went "ding," sweat sprouted out of my forehead as I pictured someone hearing that back at the entrance. I ran in the elevator and squeezed myself into the corner by the controls, first pressing the third-floor button and then repeatedly jabbing Close Door until it finally cooperated.

I was pretty sure Ben must be on the third floor of our small local hospital, since I'd seen signs saying labs and x-rays were on the first floor, and maternity on the second. Fortunately no one paid any attention to me when I stepped out of the elevator. It apparently was not anyone's job to look for intruders up here; that was the responsibility of the first-floor folks. If you made it to the third floor you were assumed to be an approved visitor.

I walked along the hall peering into rooms. Some patients were sleeping, but those who were awake looked like they were under the influence of the water. I got a sinking feeling inside, resigning myself to Ben either being in a coma or a state of stupefaction, with there being little difference between the two. He'd been one of the first to befriend me when I entered high school hardly knowing anyone. I'd lived in Los Patos all my life, but Mom had insisted on home-schooling me until I got old enough to stage a rebellion. Ben was really into tech and so was I after finally getting the chance to use computers at school. I had more in common with him than with any other friend, including Giselle, who was a lot more girlie girl than I would ever be. Which meant I would do whatever it took to spring Ben from this hospital and return him to normal, even a repeat of the Myles episode if it came to that. But I was getting ahead of myself. If we managed to bust out of Los Patos tonight and find help on the other side, we might not need to kidnap anyone again. Maybe, just maybe, we'd come riding home with the posse.

Names were written outside the doors, and when I neared the end of the second corridor, I spotted Ben's. I peered into the room and nearly gagged at the odor, which reminded me of the time a rat had died under our floorboards. An old man with wisps of hair crossing his otherwise bald pate sat in a reclined position with his eyes closed. He had a large protrusion on his neck, about the size and shape of an egg. I thought it might be a swollen lymph node, which I knew was a sign of infection. It had happened to Mom once, though hers had been smaller.

I entered the room trying not to breathe and headed toward the second bed, which was blocked by the curtain, when suddenly the man leaned forward and let out an enormous sneeze. *Eww.* Snot flew all over me, including my face.

What if he has the plague? I looked around frantically for antiseptic wipes without seeing any. *What kind of a hospital is this?* I ran into the bathroom, turned on the water full blast, and lathered my hands and face in antiseptic soap.

"Who are you?" a young male voice said.

I looked up to find an orderly at the door, gazing at me with cold, blank eyes. The man would've been handsome if any emotion showed through in his expression.

"I'm... I'm Ben's sister. I came to see how he's doing," I said, trying to keep the inflection out of my tone. "Does that man have the plague?"

"The plague?" The orderly looked puzzled. "I can't speak to you about any patient's condition. That would violate the privacy law."

"I just figured. I mean, the town's under quarantine for the plague. I thought everyone in here must have it."

"No one has told me about the quarantine," he said.

I knew it! If hospital employees knew nothing about the quarantine, there was no plague, it was just an excuse to keep us isolated. Whoever was behind it wasn't even putting much effort into keeping up a pretense. Well at least I could breathe easily now—except for the horrible stench—and it was kind of a relief to have it confirmed that no one was about to die of plague, bubonic or otherwise.

I stepped past the curtain to Ben's section of the room as the orderly went out. Ben was completely buried under what looked like several blankets and appeared to still be connected to the IV. But my hopes sank at the sight of the giant plastic cup of water, half empty, sitting on his tray.

I moved closer. "Ben?"

No response came. I walked around to the other side of the bed to try to get a glimpse of him. "Ben?" I said a little louder. Still no movement from him at all.

I touched what I thought must be his shoulder and shook him. "Ben!"

His shoulder felt too soft. I drew back the blankets to get a better look, and that's when I discovered that the shape I thought to be Ben was nothing more than a pile of pillows. My friend was gone. He had already made his escape.

Chapter Twenty-Six

Giselle and Randy did their part blocking the view again as I slipped back into the bathroom from the hallway. A minute later I came out and approached them, loudly complaining about the chili I supposedly had for lunch, which made Giselle roll her eyes and Randy look ill. But it wasn't necessary to make an excuse since the front desk person showed zero interest in the amount of time I had spent in the bathroom.

After we went out, Randy said he wanted to check on his grandmother, and I said I would go to Ben's house to find him, and then I wanted to look in on Mom. Giselle decided to stick with Randy, probably because, unlike me, he looked like he could protect her, and also his plan involved a car whereas mine relied on bike transportation. I didn't blame her; she always drove to school and wasn't used to bicycling everywhere like I was.

The front door of Ben's house was locked when I got there. Maybe they were on to my habit of walking right in. Or maybe the parents were at work and the kids at after school care. I waited ten minutes, during which time I rang the bell repeatedly and pressed my ear to the door without hearing anything, not even the drone of the ever-present infomercial. Where was Ben? Why did he sneak out of the hospital if not to come home? Most importantly, was he on to the great water caper?

I rode home next, carefully scoping out our house and driveway before riding my bike down the hill to the carport. The pickup was gone, meaning Mom must not be home, so I retrieved the spare key from where we kept it under a box. This time Mom had remembered to lock the door on her way out. Oddly, there was a copy of the Xbox version of Call of Duty sitting on the stoop. I picked it up and opened the case, looking for a note of any kind, but there was nothing. It must've been Ben who brought it, but why? Maybe it was just meant as a sign he'd been to my house, but I sure wished he'd written a message. That seemed like one more skill my generation had never picked up, because who needs to leave notes on paper when you can text a person instantly?

I let myself in. "Mom?" I called out, not expecting any reply, and not getting one. She was probably out doing her job of trying to convince stores to take her clothing on consignment. I tried to see it as a good sign that she wasn't just sitting like a zombie in front of the TV.

Part of me wanted to stay till Mom returned, grab her, and bring her to the wine cellar to wean her from the water, like we did with Myles. But that would set back our attempt to gather help from the next town by at least twenty-four hours. In my mind, we'd already delayed this action for too long.

I also didn't think I should hang around my house longer than necessary, in case the cops were checking on us like before. I jogged up to my room and changed out of the clothes Giselle had loaned me to replace the stuff I stole from Ben. My own shirt and pants that had gone through the river had turned stiff and stinky after they dried. But Giselle's figure was curvier than mine and I was sick of feeling inadequate for not filling out her clothes as completely as she did. It felt good to pull on some comfy leggings, a cotton crop top, and my favorite long, soft hoodie, plus my other sneakers that hadn't been ruined by my swim.

I hurried back downstairs and went out the back door to check on Brisa. There was plenty of hay in her pen, and her water dish was mostly full. I considered bringing filtered river water from the house, but as soon as Mom returned Brisa would be back on the hose water we usually gave her, so there wasn't any point. Brisa lay near the gate looking forlorn. I sat beside her, smoothing her fur and kissing her soft head. She was so listless she hardly seemed to notice me. All I could think was that whoever was responsible for the water had gone too far in drugging poor innocent animals. I put my arm around her and lay my head on her shoulder. "I'm going to stop the monster who's doing this if it's the last thing I do," I whispered in her ear. "I won't let them get away with it."

Cuddling with Brisa brought me back to the worst day of my life, when I was six. Usually Mom got me up, but this time she still had not come by the time the sun's morning rays hit my eyes while I lay in bed. I stumbled to my feet and ran downstairs to see where she was.

Mom was hunched over the kitchen table, her eyes red and swollen from crying. "Oh, Sierra," she said, gathering me into her arms. She burst into tears again.

"What's wrong, Mommy?"

She answered after her weeping subsided. "Papá isn't coming back."

"What? No… he said he would. He promised!"

"I know, sweetie. It isn't his fault. Something happened. Papá… isn't with us anymore."

"You mean… he went to heaven?" We weren't a religious family, despite that my father had been brought up Catholic. But I knew a boy whose mother had died, and that was how they spoke of it.

"Heaven, sure, I guess." Mom was not about to argue for atheism at the moment.

I remembered feeling stunned and drawing away. I was furious at her for telling me something so awful. It was a hateful lie, I told myself. I ran outside to Constanza's pen—she was our first goat—and buried my face in her fur. It seemed like hours before I could get myself to let go of her and return to the house.

When I was older, I learned that after my father had sworn at Mr. Franks, the horrid man reported him to the Immigration Service for being illegal. Dad got deported to El Salvador and applied for a waiver to come back. Since he'd been married to Mom for nine years, they would've granted him the waiver too. But while he was waiting, he was killed… an innocent victim caught in the crossfire of rival gangs.

Tears rolled down my cheeks. I wouldn't ever forgive myself. *I killed my father for a Snickers bar.* Remorse was a powerful motivator, though. I had followed Mom's rules for Papá's sake. Worked hard in school and prepared to go to college for Papá's sake.

And now I would battle the evil that had overcome our town… for Papá's sake.

I wiped my damp face fiercely. *Nope, not giving up yet.* I shook myself off and gave Brisa one more kiss before standing. I hated going without seeing Mom, especially since we were leaving town tonight, but if I saw her it would just be frustrating since I could do nothing for her in the short term.

Heading out on my bike, I decided to swing by Myles' place and see how he was doing with his dads. I figured after that we could go together to meet up with Giselle and Randy.

I heard the smash of his foot against the soccer ball from his front door. I let myself into the backyard from the gate, where I avoided looking up at the cracked window I still hadn't told Myles about. Or maybe he remembered it was me and it was just one more item on the long list of my offenses.

Seeing me, Myles walked over from the net where he was collecting his ball.

"How are your dads?" I said.

"Not home. I guess they're at work," he said. "Let's go in the house."

He led me to the kitchen and started taking out ingredients for sandwich-making. "You're a vegetarian, right?"

I nodded. "I'll make my own. Got peanut butter? And a banana?"

He threw me an odd look but stopped short of questioning my eating quirks. He presented me with peanut butter and a banana, which I made into a sandwich while he assembled his own out of turkey and sliced cheese. At this point my stomach was groaning because I'd skipped lunch.

"We're gonna stop this thing," I said, trying to sound more confident than I was. "We just need to get help. Whoever's behind this won't be any match for the National Guard."

Myles nodded with a distracted look. "Hey," he said. "Sorry for being a jerk."

"I don't blame you. I feel the same. In some ways it would be better to be stupefied... better not to have to be the ones to fix this for everyone."

"Yeah." He brushed his hand against my arm and smiled at me. "But it's okay. We'll get out of here tonight."

We heard a car outside and then the garage door opening. We both glanced at the window. "It's my dad." He took another bite from his sandwich.

I was a little nervous waiting for him to enter. The stupefied made me uncomfortable. Maybe it was because with a normal person, you could get an idea what they were thinking or feeling from the way they looked at you. But those who were drugged by the water spoke without any emotion and conveyed nothing with their faces. You couldn't tell what was going on inside their heads, if anything.

We watched as the door came open from the garage and an android walked in. Not Principal Droid. This one was clearly meant to be Mr. Kaneko.

Chapter Twenty-Seven

The android said, "Hi, Myles." To give the thing credit, it sounded way friendlier and more animated than any of the stupefied.

I looked at Myles. His mouth hung open and his face was drawn in horror.

The droid acted as if everything was normal and set down the briefcase it was carrying. I followed Myles' stare to Mr. Kaneko's initials stamped on the leather. This really was his dad's briefcase.

"Where's my father?" Myles' voice was low and harsh.

Robot Mr. Kaneko smiled as if he'd told a joke. "I'm your father, Myles. You know that."

"Where is my father?" The way Myles said it made me want to hide under the table.

The droid walked toward the sink. "Let me get you some water."

Myles leapt on the thing pretending to be his father and knocked it to the floor. "What did you do with my father?!" he roared into the robot's face. Myles grabbed it by the shoulders and slammed it against the tile.

The droid was not ruffled. It flexed its back muscles, pressed its hands against the ground, and flung Myles off using the force of its body. It flipped itself around and clutched Myles' neck with one hand, lifting him up as it rose onto its feet.

Myles was choking and sputtering.

"You'll feel better after you've had some water," the droid said calmly. Myles flailed his fists and landed some blows that looked like they hurt Myles more than the machine.

So far the droid had not even acknowledged my presence. Once again, I found myself searching for a weapon and cursing for not having adjusted to the new reality that I needed to be armed at all times, from now on.

I considered grabbing a knife from the butcher block, but I didn't think a knife would have any effect. The droid's body looked too hard, it would be like stabbing a statue. I tore open the cupboards and drawers, but nothing seemed heavy enough.

Looking back, I saw the droid still had Myles' neck clenched in its powerful fist. It turned on the water with its free hand and lowered Myles' face toward the tap.

I noticed it then. The fire extinguisher. I tore it down from its place near the stove.

Myles was struggling not to let water get into his mouth.

I came up behind them, raised the extinguisher, and brought it down hard on the droid's head. A spark and a bit of smoke came out of its nose, but it kept its grip on Myles' neck.

I struck again and again. After the fifth blow, Myles managed to wrench the droid's fingers off him. The thing hovered for a few seconds before falling sideways onto the floor. Its head was dented but its eyes were still open.

"Run, Myles!" I shouted, throwing down the extinguisher. Myles followed me outside to the front of the house, where we leapt on our bikes and rode off. I headed away from the center of town, toward one of the more secluded neighborhoods so we wouldn't attract attention. Eventually I turned onto a dirt road that led to somebody's ranch. We stopped and dismounted near a row of trees that would hide us from passersby.

Myles burst into tears. I didn't have any brothers so I'd never seen a teenage boy cry before. He reminded me of a wild beast after getting shot but not killed, all manic fury mingled with anguish. He shouted, stomped, and shook trees until finally throwing himself on the ground. I sat beside him, wrapped my arm around his shoulders, and drew his head to my neck, where he wet it with more tears. "They killed my father," he said in a strangled voice.

"No. We don't know that. They're holding him somewhere. I'm sure of it." I wasn't at all sure of it, but I had to give Myles hope.

"Then I have to find him."

"We don't know where to look. Even if we did, it must be guarded. We need to follow the plan. We're leaving Los Patos after dark and going for help. We'll be back with the troops tomorrow. They'll get to the bottom of this."

Myles struggled to pull himself together. After a minute, he wiped his face on his sleeve. "Okay. You're right. That's what we have to do."

I nodded and formed an expression of what I hoped looked like firm resolve. But inside I was thinking the same fate could've happened to Mom. She hadn't been home, she could've been kidnapped or worse. *No!* I refused to let these fears keep me from functioning. The plan was the same. *Leave town. Get help.*

"There's something else we need to do before we go," I said.

Myles stood and gave me a hand up. "What is it?" he said.

"We have to find Ben. And now I think I know where he is."

Chapter Twenty-Eight

I wondered if stupefaction could rub off on someone. I should've realized right away what Ben meant by leaving the Xbox game at my door. His clue said, *I'm hiding out at the video game store where I work.* He didn't want to write it down in case the wrong person—or droid—read his note and came after him.

Myles and I rode our bikes to the strip mall where *Games, Games, and More Games* was located. The place was deserted; apparently all the smaller stores that didn't sell necessary items like food were being shuttered. A CLOSED sign also hung in the liquor store window. The stupefied had no need for alcohol or any other drug beyond what they were getting in the water. Still, these closures were odd given the compulsion to do one's job, but maybe a lot of people were moving on to other jobs.

After we pedaled into the alley behind the building and ditched our bikes out of sight, I knocked on the back door of the video game store. We waited a minute, and when it didn't open, I said through the crack, "It's me. Sierra."

Ben opened the door. His injury was swollen and he wore a bandage over it on the right side of his head, just below the locks of tousled curly blond hair. Otherwise he looked like normal, except for the furtive look in his eyes as he glanced past us into the alley like he was checking for bad guys.

He looked surprised to see Myles and mumbled a "hey bruh" in his direction before telling us both to come inside quickly.

We did as he said and he shut the door fast behind us. We followed his short, rapid steps into a small back office with a desk and chair. Myles went to the corner and sat on a safe. I could tell he was still thinking about his father.

"You know it's the water, right?" I said to Ben.

"I didn't know. But when I woke up in the hospital, I had these weird memories of sitting around in a fog watching TV and guzzling water. And then, the thing that freaked me out... a droid doctor checked my vitals. She had a white lab coat and a stethoscope and the nurse kept calling her Dr. Chavez. After that, I didn't eat anything they gave me. The nurse kept bringing me Slurpee-sized glasses of water and trying to get me to drink them. I pretended to fall asleep and then later I dumped the water down the sink. Since I was still on the IV, I wasn't really thirsty anyway. This morning I felt a lot better and decided to make a decoy and get the frick out of there."

"Nice, I saw that. Everyone's stupefied except us, Giselle, and Randy," I said.

Ben snorted. "Stupefied? Good name for it. Have you seen any droids?"

"We've seen two." I didn't want to cause Myles further pain by naming them. I snuck a glance his way, but he was staring at the floor.

Ben ran his hand through his hair. "They're replacing us. That's what this is. I knew it would happen someday. But not like this."

"If so, they're not doing it very well. They don't look like us. Not really."

"I know," he said. "No one's going to believe they're people. Except the stupefied."

He walked around to the other side of the desk, facing an open laptop. "Look at this."

I followed him over there. Myles got up reluctantly and stood where he could see.

113

Ben sat down and started typing on his keyboard. "I went home first and recorded one of the videos they keep playing on TV. I wanted to figure out why they're showing it, and why people want to watch it."

He played the video on his computer. A strange-looking middle-aged woman appeared at the top of one of those sweeping staircases only found in mansions. Tall and emaciated, she had shoulder-length silver-blue hair that hung like beaded strands of plastic. She wore a clingy, shiny blue dress and silver boots. The woman spoke as she began descending the stairs. "Good evening, Duckies," she began. Los Patos means "the ducks," but none of us liked it when outsiders poked fun at the town name.

Ben pressed fast forward.

"No, wait," I said. "I haven't seen this one."

"It's so random. They added it recently." He paused, rewound, and continued playing the recording.

"My name is Demetria Moon and I'm the CEO of Pardize Industries," the woman said.

She looked as likely to be CEO of a tech company as Captain Lech was to be chief of our police force. It couldn't be a coincidence; the two weirdest people in town had to be in league with each other. Whatever was going on, I was sure they were behind it somehow.

A guy half her age, wearing a tuxedo and looking like the centerfold of *Man Beautiful*, hurried up the steps and handed her a glass of champagne. She drained the glass before tossing it over the balustrade, where it shattered on the floor below. "I generally avoid temptation unless I can't resist it," she said in a different voice, while eyeing Mr. Hot.

"She's imitating Mae West," Myles said. "A movie star from the 1940's or something."

At my surprised look, he mumbled, "My dads like her."

114

At least it wasn't me making another stereotypical assumption.

The man took her hand and led her down the stairs into a magnificent ballroom. She paused to address the camera. "Soon Pardize will transform your miserable little town into the utopia of our design. You're welcome. Until then you may watch me dance."

As ballroom dance music played, the mismatched couple whirled around the room.

"The dancing goes on for the next ten minutes," Ben said. He fast-forwarded the video again. "Whatever drug they put in the water, it must make people easy to brainwash." He stopped it and began going through frame by frame. After a few seconds he jabbed the keyboard. "Here!"

He'd stopped on a photo of a desert, with a cloudless sky, a blazing sun, and unending white sand. In the center of the picture there was a table in the sand. A glass of water rested on top of it, and not just any glass of water, but the most refreshing-looking water I'd ever seen, with ice cubes inside and dew drops all over, as if it had only just arrived from refrigerator to table. I became intensely aware how dry my throat was and how desperately I needed a drink.

I turned to Ben who gave me a knowing look and then handed out water bottles to Myles and me. "Yeah, it makes you frickin' thirsty," he said. "The video's full of these frames, but they flick on and off so fast you can't see them with your conscious mind. They play to your subconscious."

He fast-forwarded to another section of the video, paused and went frame by frame again. He stopped on an image of a blank page with writing on it. The sentences, arranged in rows, said, "Watch TV… Don't Ask Questions… Do Your Job… All is Well."

"Oh my god," I said.

"This one appears over and over in this section. Here's the last one I found…." Ben went back to fast-forwarding while I guzzled water from my bottle.

"There," he said.

It was a photo of Robot Mr. Meena, smiling above a caption that identified him as "Principal Sanjay Meena of Los Patos High School."

"There are more of these too. The doctor I saw, and…." Ben stopped, shooting a nervous glance at Myles.

"My dad," Myles said.

Ben nodded. "Sorry, man."

"Fuck," Myles said.

"Just what we thought," I said. "They're brainwashing everyone."

"It's called subliminal messaging," Ben said. "Don't watch this shit. It might affect us too, though it works best on the stupefied."

"We're getting out of here tonight," I said. "Through the Starke Lake trail."

"I'm not going," Ben said. "Can't leave my fam."

"It's just to get help," I said.

"We don't know if this is happening all over. What if we can't get back?"

I didn't know what to say; it had been on my mind as well. I briefly considered staying with Ben, but just as quickly rejected the idea. Our situation was too dire. We needed help desperately and it would be easier to convince the authorities if there were four of us vouching for the same outrageous story.

Ben opened the top drawer of the desk and got out a gun. "Take it." He lifted it gingerly like he thought it might explode in his hand. "My boss kept this here in case of burglars."

I felt a burning in my throat and a bitter taste filled my mouth. The gangsters who murdered my father had used guns.

To my surprise, Myles reached over and took the weapon from Ben. He glanced down at it and then back up. "The magazine?"

Ben looked puzzled. He bent and reached deeper into the drawer. His hand emerged with a clip full of bullets.

Myles put the gun in one pocket and magazine in another.

"Where'd you learn about guns?" I said.

"Zack taught me. His dad's a gun nut."

"Zack on the wrestling team?" At Myles' nod, I made a mental note to un-stupefy Zack—or maybe his dad—if we didn't get rescued soon.

"Sure you don't want to keep it?" I said to Ben.

"Got enough to worry about without shooting off my toe," he said.

"What's your plan?"

Ben hesitated. "Find out more about the new tech company. Pardize."

Chapter Twenty-Nine

Ben was adamant about staying behind. I stopped arguing with him when I realized it was getting dark outside and we were going to be late for meeting Randy and Giselle.

"I've got your bike," I told him. "I'll leave it here."

"Oh, that's where it went," Ben said. "Hey, did you rip off my backpack and some of my clothes too?"

I smiled at him. I didn't think most other guys would have noticed the missing clothes. He probably had an ordered list somewhere. "You'll get them back," I said.

After we left, I told Myles to ride ahead to Giselle's house while I walked in that direction. She could pick me up on the way to the lake. I figured we could leave the car there and if it was found, it wasn't the end of the world. When school started tomorrow they would know which kids were missing anyway.

But Myles, who watched a lot more horror films than I did, insisted that trouble always begins when the characters split up. "We stay together," he said, leaving Giselle's dad's bike next to Ben's behind the store.

We set a brisk pace heading toward Giselle's house. We avoided Pine Boulevard in the center of town, but Sampson Street, running parallel to the main road, was busier than we would've liked. Since it was early yet, there was moderate car traffic and even some other pedestrians.

After ten minutes or so of walking, I heard a car slowing behind us. I squeezed Myles' elbow and got ready to bolt if it was the police. Now was not the time for an encounter with Captain Lech. But a glance to the side revealed the car was a Zipi.

The Zipi pulled up beside us and its passenger window rolled down. The inside of the car was empty. A cultured male voice emerged from the car's speakers. "May I offer you a lift?" He sounded like Batman's butler. "Rides are complimentary. No tip required either," the voice added.

Before I could say anything, Myles had opened the back door and gotten in. "C'mon," he said.

"No," I said. "It's a bad idea." A Zipi was not much different than an android on wheels, and I wasn't feeling great about androids at the moment.

"It's just a car," he said, looking annoyed.

I wasn't so certain about that. "I think we should walk."

"Would you just get in?" Myles said.

I guess because I was feeling terrible about his dad, I got in the Zipi and shut the door. A second later, the seatbelts fastened automatically over us. This gave me bad feeling number two.

"Where may I escort you?" Zipi asked.

I poked Myles to keep him from answering. "I'll give you directions," I said. My plan was to stop down the street from Giselle's so it wouldn't have a record of our exact destination. "Turn right at the next light."

Myles leaned back in the cushy seat. I had to admit these cars were extremely comfortable. I had ridden in a Zipi once before. Mom had forbidden me from getting into them, but Giselle and I had been coming home from a party plastered and I figured it was the best alternative.

When a soft buzzing sound came from the seat, I realized it had warmed up and was starting to massage our backs and butts. Damn, now I would never want to get out of the car.

"Help yourself to water," Zipi said.

We glanced to the side and saw water bottles in the cup holders. Myles looked at me, but I shook my head. Even though it was in a bottle, I didn't think we should trust it.

When the red light switched to green, we turned left.

"I told you to go right," I said.

"Did you? My deepest apologies," Zipi said.

"You can make a U-turn up there," I said, wondering how the car could've mistaken my "right" for a "left." The words didn't sound alike.

"Thank you, miss," Zipi said.

But when we got to the intersection, the car continued straight.

"Where are you taking us?" I said.

"In this direction," Zipi said.

Myles and I exchanged a worried glance. "Play us some loud music," I told Zipi.

"What kind?" the distinguished voice asked.

"Anything."

A country music song began to twang.

"Louder," I said. Zipi raised the volume. I leaned over to Myles and whispered, "We're headed toward the police station."

Myles looked at me and nodded. A minute later, we came to a red light and stopped. "Now!" I yelled at Myles. I tried to snap open my seatbelt, but it was locked in place. Myles had the same problem. "Release our seatbelts!" I shouted at Zipi.

"For your protection, the seatbelts shall remain in place until we reach your destination," Zipi said.

"We want to get out here!" I said.

"We have not yet reached your destination." The light changed green and Zipi started up while I continued struggling with my seatbelt.

Blam! Zipi's front panel exploded from a gunshot.

"What the hell?!" I screamed, my ears ringing and my nerves shattered.

Myles was holding the gun. The loud music must've covered the sound of him snapping the magazine into place.

The Zipi drifted to a stop in the middle of the road.

"C'mon, let's go," Myles said.

Our seatbelts came off, but when we tried the doors, we couldn't open them. "Unlock the doors!" I shouted, in case Zipi still had any of its powers left.

"For your protection, the doors will remain locked until we reach your destination." Zipi spoke in a comically distorted deep voice that drifted off at the end.

Myles pulled me next to him, and I swooned for a second thinking it was an embrace. "Cover your face," he said.

Oh shit.

A second later, *blam!* He shot out the side window. It splintered into a thousand pieces, but at least it was safety glass so the pieces weren't sharp. We kicked at the window with our feet until the opening was wide enough for us to climb out.

Three other cars had stopped and the drivers were watching us. Several pedestrians as well.

Myles and I looked at each other. Words weren't necessary. We started to run.

Chapter Thirty

Myles veered into McLawson Park with me right behind him. If you ever go on the run from the law, make sure it's in your hometown so you know all the shortcuts. We ran around the play structure, across the basketball courts, and through the picnic area to reach the next street over. We crossed the road and cut through someone's yard to reach White Horse Lane on the other side. I got a shot of adrenaline hearing the whine of sirens starting up in the distance.

Still, I was having trouble keeping up with Myles. After all, he was a sought-after future college soccer player, while I was typically the last person picked for the kickball game. Though the last couple of days were definitely causing my muscles to tone up, and maybe, if I ever got to play kickball again, I might finally appear to be a decent prospect for the team.

He was ten yards or so ahead of me, and I could guess where he was going to detour again, but until we reached that spot we were exposed to traffic. I freaked at the sight of headlights approaching behind me and started into someone's yard. Brakes screeched and car doors opened. I sprinted to the homeowner's fence, grabbed the latch to yank the gate open, but it held fast. I was trapped.

"Sierra!" Giselle called out from behind.

I nearly collapsed in relief. Giselle ran up behind me and I threw myself into her arms. "Thank god," I breathed into her shoulder.

She patted my back. "It's okay, sweetie."

"Hurry up!" Randy shouted from beside his granny's Prius.

Giselle and I pulled apart and dashed to the car. Myles was running toward us; he must've paused to look for me. We all got in and Randy jammed his foot on the accelerator, but in a Prius, that doesn't result in any sort of dramatic speeding up.

"We looked all over for you guys," Randy said, his tone a rebuke.

I explained how we found Ben at *Games, Games, and More Games*. "A Zipi tried to kidnap us," I added at the end, realizing that sounded nearly as delusional as the Skeleton Man episode. "We had to break the window to get out."

"We drove past it," Randy said. "Figured it was you."

Of course. It seemed like I was now connected to every psychotic episode that happened in this town.

Randy took the back roads to Starke Lake and parked behind some trees. If the car was found in the morning that would be okay, but we didn't want anyone seeing it and coming to look for us tonight. We all got out and grabbed backpacks that Giselle and Randy had filled with supplies and stashed in the trunk of the car. I was particularly impressed they'd remembered to pack flashlights, considering all of us typically used our phones for this purpose. Now we could save our phones' batteries in the hope of getting service in Wilder.

We hurried over to the trailhead. The park was typical California: rolling hills covered in scrub grass, with the occasional oak tree to break up the monotony. The grass was yellowish-brown most of the time, until the arrival of the rainy season, when everything turned emerald green for a while. It was like that now. February was always the prettiest month of the year.

The trail circling the lake was flat and easy to follow for the most part, though there were plenty of stones that some less coordinated people—*cough*, me—might trip over if they weren't careful. I was grateful for the flashlights on this overcast night, but at the same time I worried they might be spotted from some distance away, given the openness of the terrain. Still, I thought we would be safe if no one had noticed our car when we turned down the road leading here. And if no one, especially not Captain Lech, guessed this might be our destination.

We got into single file with Myles in the lead, followed by me, Giselle, and Randy at the back. It seemed kind of sexist to me, with the guys protecting us front and rear, but given they actually were bigger, faster and stronger than us—since Giselle was no athletic marvel either—it kind of made sense. If we had to convert any more people, I put it on my mental list to go after Bridget, MVP of the Los Patos High School girls' basketball team.

Myles pulled ahead of us quickly, and when the trail widened a bit, Giselle drew up beside me. "He seems upset," she said, nodding toward Myles.

I filled her in on his dad, and then I told her about Ben and what he'd found embedded in the video.

Giselle shivered and drew her jacket closer around her. "I can't wait to get to Wilder so I can call my parents."

"Yeah," I said, though inside I didn't share her confidence. Things were so bad here, it was hard for me to believe Wilder could be any better. If our neighboring town was normal, why didn't anyone notice what was happening in Los Patos?

Giselle caught my mood. "Oh god, you're thinking about your mom... just plug my mouth with a shoe," she said.

"It's okay. I'm not jealous your parents aren't affected." I said that for her sake. I actually wasn't one hundred percent convinced that we'd find them unaffected. "I want everything to be normal on the other side. We can't fight this ourselves."

Giselle put an arm around me and squeezed my shoulder. "I'm so glad we're doing this. Everything's going to be all right now. Of course we'll get help. Los Patos is just one stupid little town."

I wanted to share her optimism, but the cynic in me kept clutching and twisting my stomach.

The trail narrowed again and we returned to single file. I could've enjoyed the walk if it wasn't for the fear of the police nipping at our heels. How hard would they work to track down the fugitives who vandalized a Zipi? I had no idea. Everything about our stupefied town was bizarre and confusing. I tried to settle my nerves by glancing out at the still surface of the lake. With no wind or rain to disturb it, it looked like an enormous black mirror. Beautiful and haunting.

Before long, we reached the far end of the lake. From there, the trail continued over a hill and into the town of Wilder. None of us was certain where the boundary was, except that it had to be near.

We paused and gathered round as if about to partake in some ancient ritual like the lighting of the fire, though in this case it was the bright flash of our cell phones that lit the sky. I said a silent prayer to the gods of 3G and 4G. But quick glances confirmed what we feared: still no signal. "It was worth a try," I said. We crammed our phones back into our pockets.

"C'mon," said Myles, clearly anxious to keep moving.

I fell into step beside him. We continued on the trail as it wound up the hill, while Giselle and Randy walked together behind us. When I glanced back I noticed they were holding hands.

I looked at Myles, thinking how handsome his face looked in profile and how much better I might feel if he held hands with me too. Our arms brushed against each other, sort of not accidentally, but he still made no effort to take my hand. I didn't think it was shyness. More likely his thoughts were far away, focused on his missing dad. I refused to take it personally. Once this was all over, if he still didn't ask me out on a real, non-mathematics date, then I would take it personally.

When we reached the top of the hill, we paused to gaze out over the valley. The town of Wilder lay in the distance. Its center was well lit, but the area surrounding it showed only sparse flickers of yellow and orange. Normal or not, we really couldn't tell from here. Wilder was just another quiet California town, with an even smaller population than Los Patos.

But to us it felt like seeing the Emerald City. Giselle turned to me, smiled, and squeezed my hand. We all exchanged hopeful glances. We were within sight of our goal.

Myles took a step forward and paused. I heard it then: a strange sort of buzzing, almost like bees, except I didn't think bees flew at night. Randy and Giselle had also stopped and were looking around.

"Down there," Randy said, pointing with his flashlight toward the valley.

We followed Randy's gesture to a small object coursing across the lower horizon, somewhat below the height where we now stood. The thing appeared to have four arms ending in pinpricks of light.

"It's a drone," I said. My gaze shifted, and I spotted two more.

Someone was watching the border between our two towns.

Chapter Thirty-One

"I say we cross anyway," Myles said.

We were standing in a row, watching the drones fly back and forth along a relatively straight line which we'd decided must be exactly where the barrier between the two towns lay. We had been watching them for five minutes and their routine did not vary.

It was hard to tell from this distance, but they looked small, maybe about the size of a hand. My guess, based on past conversations with Ben, was that they used thermal imaging to see in the darkness. I had a feeling these were state-of-the-art machines.

"Dude, seriously?" Randy looked at Myles. "The drones are watching for a reason. Whoever's operating them… they see us, they're gonna come after us."

"By the time they drive their jeeps out here, we'll be long gone."

"They might have a helicopter."

Giselle, ever the peacekeeper, said, "We can try crossing somewhere else. Keep walking along the edge until we find a place that's open."

"They're not going to be that careless after taking all this trouble to keep us in," Randy said. "I say we go back while we still can and work on a plan B."

"I can't go back," Myles said. "I've got a fucking robot in my house pretending to be my father."

Randy stared at him. He was the only one who hadn't known this little detail. "Shit," he said.

Something occurred to me. "Isn't your dad on the city council?" I asked Myles.

"He's city manager. Why?"

"What does he do exactly?"

"Who cares?"

"Please."

"He's in charge of running the city. The budget. Improvements. Services. He oversees everything."

"I think that's why he was picked," I said. People in positions of responsibility seemed to be going first. It gave me hope that Mom might still be safe.

"Who cares? What matters is it happened." He drew the gun from his pocket.

Randy's gaze sharpened. Giselle let out a small gasp.

"I'll take the drones out," Myles said.

"Look, man, I'm sorry about…," Randy said. "But it's not going to help. You think they won't come if their drones go dark?"

"I'm not turning back," Myles repeated.

"Myles," Giselle said, stepping between them. Her eyes were full of tears ready to overflow. "I want to leave just as badly as you. It's killing me to say this, but I agree with Randy. If they see us, they're going to stop us, and then what? We'll be drugged like the rest." She wiped her eyes roughly with the back of her hand. "We need to go."

"She's right," I said softly. "The drones might've noticed us already."

Myles took my hand and squeezed it. He lowered his head beside mine and whispered, "Trust me." His lips brushed my cheek.

Randy watched curiously, but I didn't think he heard what Myles said.

An instant later, before I grasped Myles' meaning, he took off running down the hill toward Wilder. He hopped from section to section, as graceful as a mountain goat.

"Come back!" I cried out, but he didn't stop. I thought about going after him, but I had no chance of catching him before he reached the drones. Not to mention I'd be flat on my face in no time if I tried doing what he was doing.

"Let him," Randy said. "He's the fastest. Maybe he's better off crossing without us. He can probably run all the way there."

"He's doing it for us," I said. "He knows he can get there quicker on his own."

"We should leave now," Giselle said. "Before they come."

But none of us moved. I think we needed to see Myles pass into Wilder territory and thumb his nose at the drones before we could turn back. We watched him race through the darkness, with the machines hovering ahead of him. That was when the question occurred to me. *Why are they flying so low?* They should've been higher. If they were, their view range would be much wider.

I didn't know the answer, and anyway my focus shifted to Myles as he stopped and took aim at the closest drone. Like Randy, I didn't think it would help to shoot it down, but I understood Myles' need to do so. We didn't know who was behind this—Captain Lech seemed more like a flunky to me and it was hard to imagine the dancing Moon woman in charge of anything. But clearly the drones served as the eyes and maybe even the ears of the evil mastermind behind everything that was happening. I silently urged Myles to pulverize the target and send a resounding F-U to our faceless enemy.

The retort of three shots echoed loudly from below. With the third one, the drone vaporized before our eyes. I cheered and raised my arms in a euphoria of joy. Randy and Giselle did the same, while Myles whooped back at us. We waved wildly at each other, sending Myles our encouragement, and our blessing.

Moral victory accomplished, he turned, pocketed the gun, and continued forward. Seconds later he reached the point where he looked like he would be passing directly under the line of drones. They had adjusted to fill in the gap left by the one that was destroyed.

An icy chill ran down my spine as I watched the drone nearest Myles pause in mid-air, breaking formation. Then, before any of us had time to figure out what this meant, the drone spurted downward directly toward Myles. It landed on his forehead, seeming to attach itself.

Blam! It sounded like another gun shot, but it was Myles who fell to the ground. The drone left his head and flew back into position.

I couldn't comprehend what had happened. Fog filled my brain and made me dizzy. *Get up, Myles, this isn't funny*, was my first thought.

Myles didn't move.

Realization exploded inside my head. "MYLES!" I screamed. My feet started to run.

Strong dark arms wrapped around me from behind and held me in place. *Randy.*

"LEMME GO!" I shouted, fighting him.

His voice was gentle but firm in my ear. "If you go there, the drone will shoot you too. We have to leave him. We have to go. Now."

Tears streamed down my cheeks. I stared down the hill at Myles, willing him to move. But he just lay there, a still, dark shape in the night.

Chapter Thirty-Two

I tore from Randy's grasp and began making my way down the hill. "He might be alive!" I called back, unwilling to believe what I'd seen with my own eyes.

Randy didn't try to stop me again. "Don't get too close!" he shouted after me.

I slid my way down the loose gravel and seized a tree trunk to stop myself while I was still several yards from where Myles lay. I took out my phone and shined the light toward him.

Blood formed an uneven circle on his forehead where the drone must've shot him. His eyes were open... glassy... empty of life. I couldn't deny the truth any longer. *Myles is dead.*

"Come back, Sierra!" Randy called out.

I slumped against the tree. What happened didn't feel real. Nothing felt real. Again it struck me that I was losing my mind, or might've already lost it. Despite these thoughts, some primal instinct urged me to save myself. *Turn back. Climb the hill. Go with Randy and Giselle.* My brain emptied of all other considerations as I dragged myself back up the slope and rejoined my friends.

Giselle had said nothing since it happened and appeared to be in shock. She and I followed Randy in numb silence as he led us a different way back toward town. If he hadn't kept his head or hadn't been familiar with the network of trails surrounding Los Patos, we probably would've returned along the original path, right into the hands of the police. Randy was the reason we made it out of there alive and uncaptured.

He also made the decision to leave his grandmother's car. Even if the cops hadn't found it, they'd probably set up a blockade on the lake access road and we would be caught trying to drive away. Instead, he took us on a longer trail that eventually came out behind our school. From there we had to hike another two miles to reach *Games, Games, and More Games.* It made sense not to return to Giselle's because when classes began in the morning, Robot Mr. Meena would quickly learn which kids were missing, and for all we knew, some droid truant officers would be dispatched to find us.

A sliver of dawn's light cut through the dark horizon as we returned to the shop. When Ben finally opened the door following several long, hard knocks, he only had to look at our faces to judge our mission a failure. We had been fresh and eager when we set out, but we came back dirty, exhausted, and emotionally shattered. The part of me that had dared to hope now felt shriveled and empty.

Randy took Ben aside and quietly told him about Myles. Strangely, Ben was angry at himself for not having guessed what might happen. "I was thinking about drones," he said, "but not the shooter ones. I should've remembered that. I read an article about them last month." He slammed his hand against the wall in frustration.

We picked up the two sleeping bags, blankets, and pillows that Ben had brought with him here, thinking at the time that I might be joining him. The small office was crowded with the desk, the safe, the minifridge, and a file cabinet, and we couldn't use the retail area because anyone could see in through the front windows, so we laid out the bedding in the back corridor. Randy settled by the rear door, with Giselle between him and me, and Ben closest to the office.

I heard some noises coming from Randy, and then a flame materialized from the flick of a lighter in his hand. He lit a small glass pipe, puffing at it, inhaling deeply. The heavy scent of weed filled the room.

He handed the pipe and lighter to Giselle and she did the same before holding them out to me. It was weird, but even though I didn't really like the smell or taste of marijuana, and I rarely smoked it... I didn't hesitate to take a hit. Even Ben joined in, although I was pretty sure he'd never had it before. He broke out into violent coughing with the first hit, but he got used to it by the time we reached the third or fourth round.

There had to be something elemental about sharing a pipe. The act brought us together at the moment when we most needed reassurance that we weren't alone and the world as we knew it had not yet come to an end.

As we neared the end of Randy's supply, Giselle began to weep. I didn't notice at first because she was so quiet. But when I turned and saw the tears streaming down her cheeks, my own grief came crashing down on me. A minute later we were hugging each other while buckets of water poured out of our eyes. I couldn't tell if the guys were crying or not, but at one point I noticed Ben wiping his nose with his sleeve.

I can't say exactly when it happened, but one moment I was crying and the next I was laughing at a memory of Myles that had popped into my head. I still had tears but hysterical laughter was coming out of my mouth. "You remember... ha, ha... the soccer game against Wilder... in 9th grade?" It was hard to spit the words out.

A sudden hushed silence followed, making me think I must've shocked them all with my insensitivity. And then, all at once, everyone was laughing. "You mean Myles...?" Giselle held her stomach.

"I wasn't there," said Ben, as if it was the funniest thing in the world not to have been there.

"It was right after halftime," I said, trying to catch my breath. "Myles got the ball and took off down the field." I had to pause to laugh some more. "From yards away, he slammed the ball into the net. You never saw a ball fly so fast by the goalie's head."

Giselle squealed with laughter. "It was our own goal!" she shouted.

We dissolved into spasms. "Myles…" I struggled to talk. "He… he looked around for his teammates. Ran up to someone and did one of those dances. It was super-involved, like he'd been practicing for months. That's what killed me. His teammate… I think it was Trevor… just stared at him. But he finished the dance."

Randy doubled over in noisy guffaws.

"At the end he looked around. He realized," Giselle burst out. "And he was mortified."

I turned to Ben. "You should've seen the look on his face."

"Everyone in the stands and on the field started laughing," Giselle added. "Both teams. The dance thing… it was just too funny."

"Myles laughed then too. He took it well. He didn't let it get to him," I said.

"He was a good guy," Giselle whispered.

Our laughter fizzled out. It didn't seem funny anymore. Ben handed around a box of tissues and we blew our noses. Everyone grew quiet. I felt exhausted.

"What's left in the food bin?" Randy asked Ben.

At once I became aware of the hollow cave that was my stomach. Ben got up and we all filed into the office. Randy found a head of lettuce and packages of American cheese slices in the mini-fridge, while Ben took out a loaf of wheat bread. We gathered around making cheese and lettuce sandwiches. I grabbed a small bottle of orange juice to go with mine before sitting on the safe to eat. The guys sat on the desk while Giselle settled into the chair.

"I wonder if we can get the stupefied to follow our commands," Randy said. "We could have an army of people doing everything we say. No one could stop us then."

"It's not that easy," said Ben. "I think it takes a lot of repetition." He whipped open his laptop and showed Randy and Giselle the video with the subliminal messaging.

"Hold on," Giselle said.

Ben paused on the image of the weird Moon woman coming down the staircase.

"I know that place. I've been there with my parents."

Lifestyles of the rich and wine-guzzling, I thought.

"It's the Zelwood Estate. Out on Silver Leaf Way," she said.

"Oh yeah," Ben said. "I know it. I wonder—"

A *bang* came from outside. We all froze and held our collective breath.

The door rattled.

"Are you sure Myles was dead?" Ben whispered into my ear.

I flinched as the image of his lifeless face flashed before my eyes. I nodded weakly.

Randy was looking around for something, probably a weapon.

Whomp! The person must've slammed into the door.

Ben bent down to open the lowest drawer of the file cabinet. I looked over his shoulder to see tools stored in there. He pulled out a hammer.

Randy, being closest to the door, took the hammer from him. Ben kept a large wrench for himself, and Giselle and I got screwdrivers. I stared at it, puzzling over how I would use it as a weapon. *Can I poke out someone's eye?* It didn't look sharp enough for that.

Randy went into the corridor. "Who is it?" he said at the door. There didn't seem to be much point in trying to pretend no one was here.

135

The door shook again. The three of us in the office peered out into the hall.

A shiver ran down my spine as Randy started to open the door. I figured he might as well; if it were the cops or the droids or even the stupefied, they could break the flimsy lock and force their way in whenever they felt like it. But if it was just one person, or droid, or cop, we could defend ourselves. Randy got ready, raising the hammer over his head. I did the same with my screwdriver.

Chapter Thirty-Three

The four of us stood poised behind the door with our tools raised, ready to whack or unscrew the intruder into submission. But it turned out no one was in the alley. Instead, we found a mangy mixed-breed of a dog that came up to Randy's knees. The dog didn't really even look at us, just stared straight ahead with a glazed expression, which probably meant it was stupefied. Though I'm not sure we could expect a dog to display a keen, penetrating glance even at the best of times.

"Shoo," Ben said.

Giselle pushed past Randy and knelt down to pet the dog. "Aren't you sweet," she said. "Come on in."

"We can't have a dog here," Ben said. "What if it barks?"

"She doesn't seem like a barker," Giselle said, checking for gender before coaxing her in. "Hmm, no collar. Poor thing is a stray."

"Does anyone else think this is a bad idea?" Ben said, looking at me.

I did think it was a bad idea. At the same time, I didn't have the heart to let down either Giselle or the dog. What good was surviving if we lost connection with our four-legged best friends?

"I bet she's hungry," I said.

We united around the dog, even Ben after his initial reservations. We gave her bottled water in a wide cup, and peanut butter on a paper plate. She lapped it up with little enthusiasm before curling in the corner and falling asleep. I stared down at her, thinking this sort of mundane existence was all any of us had to look forward to. Unless we fought back.

Giselle moved her bedding so she could lay her arm over the sleeping pooch. "I'm going to call you Peanut," she told the dog. No one, especially not Peanut, had any objections.

We were well into morning now but shutting the door between the corridor and the retail area kept our section relatively dark. We all lay back down to try to sleep. In my case, thoughts kept intruding and preventing me from nodding off.

"Why don't we go to the water treatment plant?" I said. "Maybe we can stop them from poisoning the water. We'd have a fighting chance if people came back to their senses," I said.

My words were met by silence, which might've just meant that everyone else had fallen asleep.

Then Randy said, "It's not going to be easy. They must be watching the place."

"It's kind of obvious what we need to do first," Giselle said.

"It is?" I said.

"You saw how ridiculous we were, trying to defend ourselves with a bunch of tools."

"We need knives," Ben said.

"No," Giselle said. "We need guns. And since this is America, it shouldn't be too hard to find some."

I would not have expected the *guns* idea to come from Giselle, but often she surprised me. She was right, of course. How many times had I already searched for an ineffective weapon? This was war. Four desperate kids—and now a dog—facing impossible odds against a huge technologically-advanced corporation and droids and Captain Lech and The Dancing Moon Woman. Not to mention Skeleton Man. We had to have guns though I still hoped it wouldn't be necessary to load them.

"Zack Puckett on the wrestling team," I said, thinking about what Myles had told me. "His father has a collection. Anyone know where he lives?"

"I know him," Randy said. "He and his mom moved out of the house a few months ago. Zack didn't want to talk about it, but rumors are going around. His dad hit his head in an accident and now he's batshit crazy."

"If he's been drinking the water he won't be a threat," Ben said. "Let's all shut up now. I need to sleep."

It made me feel better to know what the next step was. I closed my eyes and listened to Peanut's gentle breathing. I pictured resting my head on Brisa and then I drifted off.

***

When we woke at the end of the day, we had a debate about who would go steal the guns from Mr. Puckett. In the end we agreed on Randy and me. I didn't want to risk Ben, who was too valuable for his knowledge of robotics. And for the last hour or so, Giselle had been suffering from food poisoning or something that sent her running to the bathroom every five minutes, leaving a stench that was beginning to seep out into the hall. For that reason alone, I was happy to be part of the away team.

We emptied two of the backpacks in the expectation of filling them with guns and ammo. Randy's pack also had snacks and a water bottle for us to share, though we hoped to accomplish our mission quickly and get right back to the video game store.

We rode the bikes for half an hour to reach Mr. Puckett's place, located in a remote area, up a windy road at the base of the Sierra foothills. We pedaled in darkness at first, until it became rare to see a house, and then we switched on our lights until coming to the drive-way. Before walking up the hill, we ditched the bikes behind shrubs.

An old pickup truck was parked alongside two junker cars next to the house. The outside front light had been left on, though the home itself was dark. Noises came from the back… music, or people talking loudly, I wasn't sure which. A plume of smoke rose from that direction as well, which explained the heavy odor of wood fire that permeated the air.

My gaze shifted to take in the front yard and the first thing I saw caused my stomach to flip. "He's got a well," I whispered to Randy.

He followed my eyes to the offending structure. "Shit," he said.

"He's not going to be stupefied. And he's not asleep either, based on the noise and the fact that he's got an outdoor fire going."

"What do you want to do?" Randy said.

"I'm not sure."

"I say if we can get in through the front door, let's do it. We can search while he's busy in the backyard."

I thought this made sense, especially since we didn't have any backup plans regarding where to find weapons. Still, if we failed here, chances were decent we could find a rifle or two at any randomly se-lected ranch house in this part of town.

I walked up to the front door and turned the knob. *Unlocked.* I si-lently cursed, because this meant we would have to go through with it. As Randy joined me, I whispered, "Maybe if we just ask him if he can spare a couple rifles?"

"And then what if he says no?" Randy said.

We'll be out of luck, I thought. *We'll have lost our chance to sneak in and steal them.*

I nodded and pushed open the door enough so we could peer in. It was dark inside, except for the flicker of red and orange flames vis-ible through the windows at the back of the house. The fire outlined the shapes of several people seated around it, and another figure standing before them.

Randy and I looked at each other. "Fast as we can go," he hissed.

We slipped into the house leaving the door ajar for a quick exit.

Once inside, I could better hear the sounds from the back patio. It was some sort of chant. A man, probably the one standing, would say something, and the others would give a response in unison. To hear them do it made the skin prickle on the back of my neck.

Randy nudged me to move on. We scrutinized every room we came to. I had to hold back a gasp as we opened the third door to looming shadows. These turned out to be hunting trophies, the mounted heads of several deer, a bear, and a mountain lion. I could understand hunting for survival, but this display of the poor victims' heads left me with a sickening aftertaste in the back of my throat.

A minute longer and we found the weapon stash inside a large closet. Everything was neatly arranged, with ammo stored alongside the guns so we didn't have to figure out what went with what. There were handguns and rifles and even an AK-47. Zack's dad really was nuts.

We stuffed all the pistols and their magazines in different pockets in our backpacks to keep them straight. We paused over the AK-47 and made a mutual decision not to take it. I was sure if we tried to use anything that powerful we'd be sure to waste some innocent bystanders, if not accidentally shoot ourselves as well.

This had been easy. We left the room and Randy raced through the front door ahead of me. But just as I was about to follow him out, I heard the chanting reach a crescendo. Curiosity got ahold of me and I glanced through the back windows. The man was turned toward the house and I got a glimpse of his long scraggly beard, which hung down over the black robe he was wearing. A woman lay stretched out on a bench in front of him. My limbs froze in place as the man raised a jagged hunting knife above her.

"Whatta we got here?" A low-pitched voice came from behind me. Whoever it was seized a hunk of my hair and yanked my head backwards, while his burly hand pressed a knife against my throat.

Chapter Thirty-Four

The man forced me outside through the rear sliding door, his knife poised at my neck, nearly cutting into me. He reeked of sweat and piss like he hadn't washed in months.

"Reverend Puck," he said to the bearded man who I figured must be Zack's father. "I caught a live one."

"*Puckett*," the supposed reverend said. "How many times do I have to say it?" He stared at me like he was imagining my head mounted in his trophy room alongside the deer.

The guy who'd captured me withdrew his knife and forced me down on a chair. He continued to lurk behind me.

My eyes shot round the patio, hoping to spot anyone who might help me. Three women and five men sprawled in chairs beside me had uncombed, unwashed hair and threadbare clothing. One of the men smiled at me, exposing a missing front tooth. The guy next to him had flames tattooed above his eyebrows. If I were to take a guess, I'd say the so-called reverend had tapped into the lowest common denominator at the nearest homeless encampment in his quest to round up a flock of followers.

The woman who lay tied to the bench next to Mr. Puckett had a similar appearance to the others. Her eyes were half-open but it looked as if she had no idea where she was, or what was going on.

Zack's dad lowered the knife he had raised over her and walked up to me. "Who are you?" he said.

Eyeing the jagged weapon in his hand, I considered how to answer before deciding the truth might be best. "Sierra Mendez. A friend of your son Zack. I came here looking for him. Is he here?"

Mr. Puckett ignored my question. "Are you a virgin?" he said.

"Excuse me?" Weirdly, I was suddenly concerned that Randy might be listening in.

He leaned his face closer to me and I got a near-knockout whiff of something disgusting on his breath. "Are. You. A. Virgin?"

Clearly a lot was riding on my answer so I hesitated. Finally I said, "No."

"She's lying!" the man who'd captured me called out.

Mr. Puckett squinted at me as if he thought he could read my mind. "I know," he said.

"What?! No! It's the truth!" I cried out. "What's this all about?"

"Need a virgin sacrifice to appease the demon gods of the under-world," said Missing Tooth, lisping a little as he wrapped his mouth around each word.

"To stop the robot apocalypse," Flaming Eyebrows added.

"Shut up," Mr. Puckett said. "Take Abigail away." He nodded at the woman who had no idea how narrowly she'd missed being skewered.

"Tol' you Abbie ain't no virgin," my abductor muttered as he and Flaming Eyebrows untied her and lifted her up. They dropped her on the floor nearby.

Mr. Puckett clenched my arm and yanked me up. I looked into his wide open, misaligned stare and reeled from the *crazy* I saw lurking inside him. With his other hand, he aimed the jagged hunting knife at my belly.

"Let me go!" I screamed.

"Tie her down," he commanded. Missing Tooth and Flaming Eyebrows each clutched a side of me and forced me flat on the bench.

Missing Tooth pressed down on me while his accomplice used ropes to bind my wrists, waist, and ankles.

"Help me! Someone, please!" I cried out to the spectators. Their glazed eyes avoided me.

"Gag her," said their leader.

Missing Tooth took a thin scarf from a woman with greasy hair and a stained coat. He tied it around my head so tight it went into my mouth. The fabric reeked of vomit, nearly forcing me to heave myself.

I struggled to loosen my bindings, but they stayed taut and unyielding. Beads of sweat popped from my forehead like rats fleeing the sinking ship that was me.

Since that awful morning when the dead body had turned up, every aspect of life in Los Patos had careened into a whirlpool of deranged goings on. For me it would all end here, in the back yard of this demented man, surrounded by his followers who were too far gone to save me even if they wanted to.

Jumbled phrases spewed from Mr. Puckett's mouth in a weird language I couldn't understand. The others chanted the words—or something like them—in response. The man waved his nasty weapon and raised his voice, calling out in harsh syllables.

Of all the possible ways I could die, I never would have guessed *virgin sacrifice to appease the demon gods of the underworld.* Even Mom, with her paranoia, could not have imagined it.

Trembling wracked my body. I squeezed my eyes shut, craving the image of Papá's face before I died. I wished for an afterlife where my father would wrap me in his warm embrace when I arrived, instead of the cold, scientific finality of transforming into nothing and no one.

Mr. Puckett's gestures grew more agitated; his speech swelled into a mad roar. Any second, he would plunge the knife into my heart.

Chapter Thirty-Five

"HOLD IT!" Randy shouted.

I opened my eyes and looked toward the house, where he was standing just outside the door. He held one of the pistols steady in both hands, and almost looked as if he knew how to use it. At least to a novice like me. In fact, he looked like a gun-totin', virgin-rescuin' angel from on high to me.

Mr. Puckett paused to glare at him.

"Let her go!" Randy said.

Everyone hesitated, until Zack's dad nodded at his flunkies, and my original abductor untied me. I stood up shakily and tore the scarf from my mouth as fast as I could.

But then Mr. Puckett grabbed me around the waist and put the knife to my neck. Man, I was sick to death of this maneuver.

"Drop the gun or I slit her throat," he said.

Blam! Randy fired a shot. For a second I was frozen in shock because, you know, that bullet could've hit me. But I recovered faster than Mr. Puckett, allowing me to slam my foot down hard on his instep and jab my elbow into his gut. His grip weakened and I broke away, dashing to Randy, being careful not to get between the gun and its target.

Blam! Blam! Blam! Randy was shooting wildly and it didn't seem like anyone was getting hit. I wondered if he only meant to scare them or if his aim was godawful. But then Mr. Puckett cried out and I looked back to see blood gushing from his thigh.

I slung my backpack over my shoulder, raced past Randy into the house, and sped outside.

Randy came only seconds behind me. We sprinted toward our bikes at the end of the driveway. As we paused to get on them, we glanced back to see my abductor emerging from the house. Randy shot two more times and the guy leapt back through the door.

We tore down the hill on our bikes. Given his bullet wound, I didn't think Zack's dad would be continuing with the sacrifice any time soon. I just hoped the poor wasted woman who'd been the first intended victim would get far away from there before Mr. Puckett healed and got back to business. With luck, they'd load him up with tap water in the hospital and he'd forget all about being a self-proclaimed reverend bent on stopping the apocalypse in the most cruel and ineffective way possible.

We had probably gone a mile at top speed before Randy pulled over by the side of the way. He was still holding the gun and needed to put it away. I stopped next to him and flung my arms around him, while he wrapped me in a tight embrace. "Thank you," I breathed.

Thinking of Giselle, I drew back before there was any chance of me feeling too comfortable in this position. From the way Randy looked into my eyes, I could tell he'd really been afraid for me.

"We better not stop." I glanced back nervously for signs of pursuit.

He gave me a smile then. "I hid their distributor caps. And cut the phone line to be sure they couldn't even make a local call. It's what took me so long. That, and figuring out how to use the gun."

I'd forgotten he had a part-time job at an auto repair shop so he knew cars well. I grabbed him again to give him a thank you kiss on the cheek, but by accident our lips met instead. We both jumped back and he mumbled an apology. I looked away.

We got on our bikes and didn't stop again until we reached the video game store.

Giselle was sleeping and Ben was flipping through a pile of tech magazines looking for references to Pardize. The experience of having nearly become a cultish sacrifice had exhausted me, so I left it to Randy to explain the insanity to Ben, while I grabbed a blanket, curled up in the corner, and fell asleep.

The dog growling woke me up. It was a vicious, deep-throated, I'm-going-to-attack-any-minute sort of growl that made me snap open my eyes. Ben was trying to calm Peanut, but she was baring her teeth at him, Cujo-style. "No!" Ben shouted. The pooch lunged at him.

Either Peanut was going through withdrawal or she was a stray with anger issues that were re-emerging now that the drugs were wearing off. In any case we couldn't take the chance of allowing her to stay inside with us. I jumped up and opened the back door. "C'mon girl," I said. "C'mon, Peanut," I added, in the hope she'd already bonded with her new name.

She leapt toward me. I jumped sideways, just avoiding her. She barked in a frenzy.

A piece of sausage flew past my head. "Go get it!" Randy said.

Peanut bolted after it and I kicked the door shut behind her.

"Phew," said Ben.

"Poor thing. She can't help it," I said. "But we can't have her attacking us either." I glanced around. "Where's Giselle?"

"In the bathroom," Randy said. "She's still not feeling good."

I walked down the hallway and knocked on the door. "You okay in there?" I said.

She opened the door. Her dark skin had paled a bit and she looked worn and exhausted.

"Hey, you want to lie down?" I said.

She nodded and sat on the blanket she'd been using. "Where's Peanut?" she said.

I explained what had happened. That she didn't insist on our giving Peanut a second chance just showed how sick she was. I felt her forehead the way my mother did with me. "You're burning up," I said. "Ben, do you have any Tylenol?"

I heard him opening drawers in the office. A minute later he came out with a couple of pills and a bottle of water. I sat beside Giselle and helped her take them. "Any idea how you might've gotten sick?" I asked.

She shook her head. "No clue." After swallowing the pills, she sunk down on the blanket and closed her eyes.

I looked at the two guys. "Might be food poisoning." Which seemed unlikely since we'd all been eating the same pre-packaged junk food. That might sicken us over time, but it would take years.

And then I remembered the supposed *plague*. My gaze shifted to Randy and I could tell he knew what I was thinking, but he gave a subtle shake to his head, meaning, don't say it. I didn't. *There is no plague. It's all a lie,* I told myself. Still, I couldn't help worry about Giselle.

The guys and I gathered in the office and shut the door in order not to disturb her.

"Dudes, we can't afford to wait," said Ben. "We need to check out the water treatment plant."

"I'll go with you," Randy said.

"No, I'll go," I said. "You should stay with Giselle. If she has to be moved, I can't carry her."

Randy thought for a second. He was a man of action and it killed him not to be going out and doing something, but my logic was undeniable. He gave us a nod.

Phew. Saved from having to tell him we needed Ben at the treatment plant because he was better at figuring out how things worked.

***

149

Ben and I set out on the bikes after dark. I knew exactly where the water treatment plant was. Thanks to Mom's feud, we had driven out there a couple times. I thought back to how this all started, with the water district manager floating down our river. At the time I'd thought it was just an accident, or at worst, a simple case of murder that obviously didn't involve my mother. But instead, it was the launch of something far more sinister. If only I could turn back the clock to the day before Mr. Delmar drowned and choose a different path for our town, one that would alter the whole progression of events from beginning to end.

We stuck to the back roads again and fortunately didn't cross paths with any police cruisers. More and more it seemed as if they were putting no effort into tracking us down. They had to be aware of us, especially after the drone incident that I refused to let myself think about. I could only conclude they had judged us as no threat whatsoever. Would you scour your house to kill a few fruit flies that had snuck in and were nibbling on your basil leaves? It wouldn't be worth the effort. That's all we were to them: fruit flies. I had to fight the nagging doubts telling me they were right to dismiss us. *A person's a person, no matter how small,* I reminded myself. *Horton Hears a Who* taught me every individual can make a difference if they try. I clutched that lesson to my heart.

We stashed our bikes within a grove of trees across the street from the road that led into the facility. The area was still and almost unnaturally quiet, so when an owl hooted a moment later it made me jump. We avoided the gravel walkway that crunched under our feet and continued along the pavement to keep from making any noise.

I began to feel hopeful. Why hadn't we tried this sooner? Now that we had guns, we ought to be able to shoot out a lock and get into the plant. It looked so easy to do that on TV. Once inside, I trusted Ben to figure out how to stop adding the drugs, or if not that, to find a way to shut down the whole operation. A few well-placed bullets could accomplish this, I thought. Then, having no tap water would force everyone to find other sources of liquid. All we needed was twenty-four or so hours to get people unhooked. Internally, I gave myself a little pep rallying call: *We can do this!*

The lights of the facility flickered in the distance. Ben and I exchanged a nervous look and slowed our pace. My shoulders grew tight.

A moment later we glimpsed the front entrance, which was well-lit from above. Eight armed soldiers formed a rigid formation in front of the gate.

On second glance, I realized they were droids.

Chapter Thirty-Six

Ben and I slipped away without a sound. No way could we take on a small army of robots. We had guns but barely knew how to use them. I didn't think either of us could hit a freight train from five feet away, and it looked like Ben felt the same.

We paused when we reached the bikes. "Pardize isn't that far," he said.

"Yeah, but they probably have Megatron posted outside there," I said.

"We might as well look. Find out what we're up against."

I wasn't convinced it was better to know. Would Jack have climbed the beanstalk if he knew a giant lay in wait for him? But I didn't feel like making the case for ignorance. We hopped on our bikes and started riding, while I struggled to stifle the butterflies banging around inside me.

Half an hour later we were climbing a hill that overlooked Pardize. Lights blazed across the massive complex. But more than that... the place hummed with activity. Reams of guards patrolled the grounds. Human or droid, we couldn't tell from this distance. Inside most of the buildings, every floor was lit up, highlighting the employees at work. Black swirls rose out of a detached, windowless factory at the far end of the complex, spreading an odor that reminded me of burnt plastic.

I wondered what was being so urgently constructed. *Probably droids.* They still had a lot of people to replace.

Ben dug into his bag and got out a pair of high-powered binoculars. Sometimes he surprised even me by how prepared he was. I leaned against a tree trying not to freak out while he carefully scanned the facility.

"Oh frickin' hell," Ben said. He handed the binoculars to me. "Building on the left, third window from the right, bottom floor." He looked spooked, like he'd just seen the Queen Mother in *Aliens* or something equally horrific.

My hands shook as I raised the binoculars to my eyes, not sure if I even wanted to see this thing. It took a minute to get focused and aim the lenses at the right window, and then I saw it. A droid hung from a bar with its feet above the ground and clamps around its head holding it in place. The droid was dressed and a man was bent over one of its feet, apparently tying its shoe. The man finished and the suspension bar took away the droid.

When the man stood and turned sideways, I gasped in recognition. *Mr. Meena.* Our missing principal. The real one, not the droid version.

The assembly line moved forward, bringing a second droid to Mr. Meena's position. This one was stark naked, answering a question I hadn't even thought to ask yet. *The robots have no junk.* Mr. Meena took a pair of boxers from a pile and slid them up the droid's legs.

His job is dressing droids. I wasn't sure why they couldn't dress themselves after being activated, but maybe they had more important things to do. *Like take over the world.*

The back of a real woman came into view. She was sweeping the area near Mr. Meena. A second later, my throat went dry as I realized who it was. She turned then, revealing her face.

"*Mom.*" My voice sounded hollow. I dropped the binoculars, while my feet set a path toward the facility.

Ben grabbed me from behind. "Sierra, you can't go there!"

A fog blew into my brain and for a minute I couldn't think. Gradually a little light crept back in and I knew Ben was right. I would not be able to rescue Mom by walking up to the building. I'd get caught and it wouldn't be long before I'd be running the vacuum beside her.

"It's good news, really," Ben whispered. "They haven't killed anyone."

He was right. Mr. Meena had been replaced, but here he was. *Alive.* Probably if I went home now, I'd find Robot Mom, a bizarro opposite of real Mom who would insist on my drinking the tap water. It was lucky I'd seen her here first, before encountering the Mom droid, or I would've been terrified that they'd murdered her.

"Talk about irony," Ben marveled. "We wanted to build robots to do our menial tasks. But they've already turned it around on us." He actually sounded impressed.

I was not impressed; I just wanted to get out of there. The need to free Mom and the others gave our quest a new urgency. "Let's go," I said.

We turned and retraced our steps to our bikes. From there, we chose a more direct route back. I was riding ahead of Ben when I happened to notice brand new construction on the side of the road where there used to be empty grazing land. The place was dark and didn't have any security around it, so I pulled over to take a closer look. Ben rode up beside me, and we both stared at the looming building, which could've been twenty stories high. I couldn't recall ever having seen a building taller than five or six floors in Los Patos.

"Apartments?" I said.

He shrugged. "Part of the new Utopia?" He got off his bike. "Let's take a look."

We ditched our bikes again and walked over to the structure. The frame was completed, but not the outer walls, so we were able to walk right in. We entered an inner courtyard where we could look up at the

154

levels rising above us. I took out my flashlight and shined it upwards. Each floor was broken up into rows of small rooms.

"What does this remind you of?" Ben's tone set off tiny alarms inside my head.

I rubbed the back of my neck as I stared upwards. It came to me then. "A prison," I said in a small voice. A scene from a movie flashed into my mind… prison guards standing in the courtyard looking up at the cells arranged in rows along balcony corridors. All these rooms needed were the bars.

"They're going to put us here," I said. "After they've replaced us."

"Yeah," Ben said.

A *clatter* came from somewhere nearby, making my heart leap into my throat. We whirled around, and Ben even whipped the gun out of his pocket. "Who's there?" he called out.

No one answered.

I flicked the flashlight back on and waved it around. We couldn't see anyone.

"We better get out of here," said Ben.

I nodded. We headed toward the exit. Footsteps slapped the concrete floor ahead of us.

"Stop!" I cried, spraying the area with the glow of my flashlight. A figure was revealed… it looked like *Skeleton Man*. Now that I got a better glimpse, I realized it was more like *Skeleton Woman*. The body had some feminine shape to it.

She ran outside.

For some crazy reason, I started after her. She wasn't that fast; her movements were measured and robotic, reminding me of Principal Droid. I kept my light on her until she ducked behind a row of Porta Potties.

Ben came up behind me. "What're you doing?"

"I've seen that… thing… before. C'mere." I went to the Porta Potties and now I took out my gun. With flashlight in one hand, and weapon in the other, I approached the back side of the toilets and peered around.

The area was empty. I waved the light all around, but Skeleton Woman had disappeared. I turned back to find Ben walking up behind me. "It's a droid. We need to get out of here," he said.

We hurried back to our bikes. On the way, I told Ben about the first time I saw Skeleton Woman, when I nearly ran into her in my car.

"Me too," he said, to my surprise. "That's how I crashed. Swerving to avoid her."

Despite the bump on his head, I'd nearly forgotten about his car accident.

Ben frowned. "She isn't like the others."

"It's like she isn't finished," I said. This time when I saw her, I realized what had looked like a skeleton was the droid's unadorned skull and frame. She wasn't covered by skin and hair like the other droids. Skeleton Woman just looked like a machine, a kind of C3PO except not so shiny.

"I wonder why she's running around town," Ben said.

"Like she's afraid of something," I said.

Ben mounted his bike. "C'mon. She's probably reporting back to her masters."

We rode to the alley behind the store. I was the first to pedal up and I knew right away something was wrong when I saw the back door had been left halfway open.

Chapter Thirty-Seven

A glance at Ben confirmed he found the open door as ominous as I did. We quietly took out our guns, with me hoping just the sight of them would convince people and droids to cooperate. If Giselle's electric toothbrush could have that effect, why not actual weapons?

I slowly pushed the door inward as we peered inside. The corridor was unexpectedly empty—blankets, pillows, and sleeping bags gone. I walked in ahead of Ben, trying hard to still the trembling of my trigger hand.

"Lower your weapons!" I shouted before stepping into the office and finding no one there. Ben checked the bathroom and retail area before rejoining me.

"They're gone," he said.

That much was obvious. More surprising was our stuff being gone too, including Ben's laptop and all the food and drink supplies.

"We should go," Ben said. "They left for a reason."

"They had nothing but Randy's skateboard. How'd they manage to take all the stuff?" I said.

Ben picked up a piece of paper left on top of the safe and read it aloud. "Little Mountain: Baby Blue Eyes." When he handed it to me, I noticed a little blue flower drawn after the words. Randy was a skilled artist, not just when it came to designing tattoos.

"He better not be talking about me," Ben said. He was the only one in our group who had blue eyes.

I laughed. "No," I said. "Now this is a good clue." I gave Ben a pointed look.

"Is that a jab at the clue I left for you? Hey, you figured it out."

"Yeah, whatevs," I said. It actually would not have been bad if I'd been thinking normally.

"So who's Baby Blue Eyes?"

"No one. It's not a person, it's a flower. I know where they are."

***

Little Mountain was a reference to me. "Sierra" means mountain range in Spanish. During the time leading up to when he asked me on the date that I broke to be with Myles, he sometimes called me Little Mountain to tease me.

"Baby blue eyes" is a type of early-blooming wildflower that grows around here. There was a certain piece of property Randy had taken me to see once, and at the time a large section had been covered in small blooms... baby blue eyes. I'd said how beautiful I thought they were.

The place was a seven-acre lot purchased by his parents before they died in a small plane crash. They'd been planning on building their dream home there. The lot was now held in trust for Randy. He would be able to sell it when he turned eighteen or twenty-one, I couldn't remember which. I thought he would do his best not to sell it, though. It was something tangible that connected him to the parents he would never get to see or speak to again.

An old cabin sat on the property near a creek. Randy's parents had been planning to tear it down before building their house. It would make a great hideout... unless the cops were looking for us, knew Randy was part of our group, and started digging into his family history. But I had a feeling if they'd been driven from the video store by the threat of police, Randy would've picked someplace else to go.

I thought my legs would fall off by the time we reached the property, after everywhere we'd already ridden during the night. Ben looked equally beat. We hid our bikes from the road and Ben followed me towards where I thought the cabin was. The smell of wood smoke led us the rest of the way. Of course, the cabin had no electricity or any other utilities, so they must've started the fire to warm themselves. We would probably need to put that out once daylight came.

Ben and I approached cautiously in case I was wrong about the clue, or wrong about this being Randy's lot. We got out our guns again before Ben knocked lightly on the door. "We're looking for friends," he said, hoping to allay fears.

Randy opened the door. "Hey, you figured it out," he said.

From the way he looked at me, I knew something was wrong. I pushed my way in and looked around.

"Where's Giselle?" I said. It was a one room place without even a bathroom, so there was no place to hide.

"Give me a second to explain," Randy said.

I turned on him. "Where's Giselle?"

"She's at the hospital."

"Why? How?"

"Maybe you should calm down," Ben said lightly.

I threw him a glare as well.

"She was delirious. I felt her forehead and she was burning up. I couldn't get her to drink anything. I thought she might die if she didn't get help," Randy said.

"What if she gets stupefied?!" I shouted into his face.

"It's better than dying!"

"I'm not sure it is!"

"Hey, hey." Ben tried to get between us. "This isn't helping. How did you get her to the hospital?" he asked Randy.

"It was your car," Randy said. "Your family's, I mean. Your dad came looking for you at the store. I never met him before, but he told me his name. He said you'd left the hospital and he was trying to find you."

Ben's face lit up with hope. "He wasn't stupefied?"

Randy exhaled heavily. "He was. Sorry. I think he just remembered that one of his *jobs* is dad. I told him you were fine but I didn't know where you were. He said he was gonna call the police to report you missing. I was afraid when he talked to them, he'd mention us being at the store."

"What'd you do?" My voice was full of accusation.

"What do you think I…? Jesus, Sierra." He looked back at Ben. "I showed him the gun. That's all. Just so we could get out of there."

"You pulled a freaking gun on my father?" Now Ben was pissed off.

"I made him carry Giselle to the back seat. Then I had him load his car with our stuff. I took his keys and left him there. Figured by the time he found a landline phone somewhere to make a local call, we'd be far enough away."

"Where's the car?" Ben said.

"After I brought Giselle to the hospital, I stopped at the all-night store and bought a lot more food and drinks. I dropped it all off here, then I drove the car, left it in some neighborhood. I skateboarded back."

"You should've stayed with her at least," I said.

He gave me a pained look. "I thought you'd need my help."

I grabbed one of the sleeping bags. "I'll sleep outside." I was frustrated and exhausted and really had no idea what to do at this point. And I didn't want to be in the same room as Randy. I left the cabin, opened my sleeping bag under a tree, and curled up inside it.

No matter how much the crackling of branches in the woods might sound like footsteps, I refused to go back inside.

Chapter Thirty-Eight

A drop of water on my cheek woke me up. It was raining lightly and the branches above were doing a decent job keeping me dry. But here and there the drips made it through to me.

I got out my phone to check how late in the day it was and to verify for the hundredth time that I had no service. It was 3:20 PM, meaning I'd had more than eight hours sleep. I wished I could nod off for another eight hours, but my stomach cried out for something to fill it.

The food was inside the cabin so that was where I would have to go. I couldn't avoid Randy forever anyway. Only three of us remained and I had no idea what we could possibly hope to accomplish, but there it was. I considered going to the hospital to check on Giselle, and busting her out like I'd been planning to do with Ben if she was feeling better. But the clock was ticking down on us. Whatever window of opportunity we might have—and it was more like an atom-sized pinprick of opportunity—I knew we would not have it for long.

"Hungry?" Randy's voice came from the direction of the cabin.

I turned to see him walking toward me with a sandwich on a plate and a bottle of red Gatorade. I sat up and leaned against the tree before Randy presented me with his offering.

If nothing else, my stomach was ready to forgive and forget. I dug into the sandwich—a peanut butter and jelly—without delay. Though I hated to give Randy the satisfaction of knowing he'd pleased me, it was difficult to suppress my pleasure in eating this food after so many hours without anything.

He sat down beside me. A raindrop splattered his nose and he wiped it away.

Swigging from the Gatorade, I suddenly noticed what I hadn't been able to see during the night. The baby blue eyes were in full bloom.

"I like this hideout better than the video store," I said.

"Yeah," he said.

"You're lucky to have this place." The minute the sentence left my lips, I wanted to shoot myself. Randy was the opposite of lucky. He owned this property because his parents had died. *I'm an idiot.* I was worse than the stupefied. At least they had an excuse for their moronic behavior.

He read my expression. "Hey, it's okay. I know what you mean."

Randy had been eight when he lost them. I thought about how devastated I'd been when we got the news my father had been killed. What if it had been Mom too? *Damn.* It was hard to stay mad at someone who'd had been through so much tragedy.

"Life is hell," I said. "Why are we trying so hard to save it?"

We stared at the early-blooming flowers clustered along the other side of the clearing and the emerald green hills beyond. A gap opened in the clouds and yellow shafts of sunlight made the damp baby blue eyes sparkle.

"This place is beautiful," Randy said. "I don't want to die. Or lose my mind."

"Survival's an instinct. That's why we're doing this. It's just instinct."

He shook his head. "There's more to it than that. Snakes and bugs and probably even the stupidest animals on the planet—say, barnacles—have instincts. We've got more than that. I don't just want to survive. I want to be happy, and I want to make other people happy. I want to do something with my life. Be special. I hope people remember me when I die. At least my own family."

I connected with everything he was saying. All this time I had been focusing on what I didn't like about him, maybe because he'd moved into the no-boyfriend zone. But now I realized what had attracted me to him in the first place. He cared about people and art and nature, and you could count on him. He kept a low profile so a lot of people didn't know that about him. Tattooed stoner skateboarder was all they saw when they looked at him. One of many high school stereotypes. But if you looked deeper, you would find this smart, kind, determined boy, who, like most kids our age, was still just trying to figure out his place in the world.

Giselle was a lucky girl.

"So what're we gonna do?" I said.

"Ben and I were talking."

"Yeah?"

"We need to go to the top."

"Huh?"

"Demetria Moon. President of Pardize."

"The dancing woman? How do we do that?"

"Remember?" he said. "When Ben showed us the video? Giselle told us where she lives."

I sat up straighter. I was a girl in need of a plan and we were getting closer to one. "Okay, so we go there. But maybe it's guarded by androids like everyplace else."

"Maybe it is," Randy said. "But it's a huge property. They can't be everywhere. Maybe there's a spot where we can slip through. We've got guns now. If we get in, we can force her to tell us what's going on."

"It's worth trying." Excitement surged through me. It was a chance. I desperately wanted answers and this could be the way.

"Let's go there tonight," I said. "Ben too. No point in separating anymore."

"Yeah. Time's running out."

Chapter Thirty-Nine

Approaching the Moon woman's mansion was easy. Too easy. My instincts told me there were bound to be obstacles; it was only a matter of time and place.

She had a gated driveway with an intercom but no security guard posted there. The rest of the property was unfenced. Ben and I rode our bikes on the grass, while Randy jogged alongside us holding his skateboard. The lawn was enormous and perfectly maintained, though it had to cost a fortune to water during the dry season. We headed toward the back of the house, where an expansive patio with views of the foothills jutted out. Light shone from a set of wide-open French doors.

We stashed our bikes and skateboard below the patio and climbed up along the side to position ourselves against the house beside the doors. Ballroom music poured out from the place. Rousing applause followed the end of a song. The three of us exchanged looks. It sounded as if half the town must be in there.

When the next tune started up, we ventured a glance inside. The Moon woman looped across the floor with the same dance partner she'd had on the video. Thankfully, there was no live orchestra, just an android in a tuxedo and a wild-haired toupee. The music appeared to be coming out of his open mouth. The "audience" consisted of roughly twelve more male and female-looking androids wearing formal attire. They stared raptly if not to say robotically at the swirling couple and gasped at every dance move as if they were watching the principals of the Bolshoi ballet. As a result, they made up one of the most appreciative and least discerning audiences ever.

What now? Sure, we could literally waltz right in, directly into the arms of a dozen waiting droids. We needed Demetria Moon alone before we could threaten her into answering our questions.

The current song ended and the robots broke into applause that was clearly supplemented by their audio systems. The number of voices shouting "magnificent," "breathtaking," and "bravo" far exceeded the number of droids in the room.

Demetria and her partner took curtsies and bows, though she seemed dissatisfied. She must've been well aware this was not a real audience and never would be. A droid dressed like a butler opened double doors from inside the house, stepped into the ballroom, and formally announced that Moon's dinner guest had arrived. Demetria dismissed her dance partner, who disappeared through the doors.

"Bozo, lock up the French doors," she said to a droid with flaming red hair. She turned toward the corridor.

Crap. We all looked at each other, not sure what to do. They were closing off our access to the house. Unfortunately, we couldn't attack this droid before it locked up, because an audience full of witnesses still sat in the ballroom. We would have to wait and smash the glass after they left the room, at the risk of being overheard.

To my astonishment, Ben leapt out in front of the opening. "Hey boys and girls!" he shouted.

My heart popped into my throat. Ben waved his hands wildly at the droids. "Bet you can't catch me!" he yelled at them. Then he shot us a quick glance and hissed, "Hide!"

Without really thinking, Randy and I dove behind whatever was nearest: a shrub in his case, the barbecue grill in mine. Ben turned and sprinted across the patio toward the lawn. He did not go in the direction of the bikes, which meant he would have to outrun the droids. I figured he didn't want them guessing there were three of us by revealing the bike/skateboard stash. But I cursed him for doing this, even though his motive was pure and he was trying to clear the way for us. How could he expect to outrun droids? He would be caught and then who knew what they might do to him.

"Catch that damn kid!" shouted Demetria Moon from inside the house. I heard the sounds of robots shooting to their feet and thundering toward the patio. From my hiding place, I glimpsed Bozo leading the cavalry out of the house toward Ben bolting across the lawn. The sight of them gave me some relief.

These were not the sort of super-fast, super-powered droids we were used to watching in the movies. As we already knew regarding their feeble attempt to replicate people, these droids were in the early design stages. They ran much as we had seen Principal Droid walking: with precise, measure steps. Like a robot, unsurprisingly. Their running speed was not much faster than their walking pace.

They'll never catch Ben, I thought with satisfaction. And now I realized, *Ben knew this*. We'd seen Skeleton Woman running, and it had been at the same pace. Ben had taken a risk, though. These might've been new, improved models that could go faster. In any case, I just wish he'd told me his plan in advance so I wouldn't have had to have a heart attack over it.

"Not all of you!" shouted Ms. Moon, but it was too late to stop the droids and the command was too vague. They would never figure out which of them she meant in saying *not all of you*. The whole gang kept going toward the place where Ben had disappeared under the trees.

I got up and moved back near the door to check where the Moon woman was. I was just in time to see her leave the ballroom, and now the place was empty. I gestured to Randy and together we entered the house.

"We need to be quick before the droids get back," I said.

"She's got someone here for dinner," Randy said. "We should listen in."

We hurried to the door, which had been left ajar. Randy glanced into the corridor, then nodded. We slipped out of the room.

Voices came from the front section of the house. It sounded as if Demetria was greeting her guest. Hearing footsteps, we ducked back into the ballroom. Peeking from behind the door, I saw a droid dressed as a formal waiter balancing a large tray of fruit with his white-gloved hands. A moment later the droid returned empty-handed, continuing back the way he had come.

As soon as he was out of view, Randy and I dashed out of the room toward where the droid had delivered the food. We came to a magnificent dining room with one side lined by floor-to-ceiling windows. The place was dimly lit by a row of candles on the long table. Two places were elegantly set, with one at the head and the other immediately to the right. At least they had the sense not to place the guest a mile away at the opposite end of the table.

Where to hide? The tablecloth reached the floor on all sides. It seemed like a comedy movie cliché, but we had no other place to go.

"There was a minor disturbance earlier." Demetria Moon's voice approached the dining room.

I lifted the tablecloth and gestured frantically to Randy. He dove under the table, and I followed after him, dropping the cloth behind me. In the darkness, I could barely make him out, sitting in a bent position, rubbing his head as if he had hit it against the wood. He really was too tall to be folded up under tables. I managed better, though I had landed with my legs arranged like pretzels and I didn't dare adjust myself in case I made a noise.

A man's voice spoke next. "A disturbance in the force? Tell me about it."

My skin went cold. I recognized the voice. It belonged to our Star Wars-quoting, Lego-loving, potentially pedophiliac chief of police. Captain Lech himself.

Chapter Forty

"Oh Irwin, it was just one of the braindead." Demetria Moon spoke in a low voice that she stretched out like a drawl. "Somehow he wandered over here and wanted to play with the droids."

It didn't surprise me that Captain Lech's first name was Irwin. Nor was I surprised to learn that the two weirdest un-stupefied people in town were in cahoots.

"They don't usually wander," Irwin said. "But some people react differently to the drugs."

From under the table, I heard footsteps entering the room. Given the uniform pace, I figured it must be a droid. I hoped it wouldn't be reporting that they caught Ben.

"Chardonnay?" the droid said.

I felt a flutter of relief.

"Yes, of course," the Moon woman said. She and Lech remained silent while the droid apparently popped the cork and poured wine into their glasses.

"Shall I pour glasses for the others, Madame?" the droid said.

Panic shot through me, lifting the hair on my arms. The droid must've heard us, probably our breathing. Dogs could hear that well, so I knew it was possible. The "others" mentioned by the droid had to be us.

I looked at Randy and though it was dark, I could see his hand reaching toward where his gun bulged in his pocket.

"What?" Demetria said, sounding distracted.

"Leave us alone," Lech barked. "Shut the door after you."

I let out my breath. Randy lowered his hand. They weren't paying attention to the droid. They hadn't understood what it was talking about.

"Was that really necessary?" Moon said.

"Hold on."

I heard a chair being pushed back. *Crap.* It looked like he *had* understood what the droid's words implied. My hand felt clammy as I pressed it against the pocket that held the gun. I looked at Randy and he was doing the same again.

"You hear that sound?" Lech said.

"What sound?" the Moon woman said.

The sound of a little girl freaking out under the table, I mentally filled in for him.

"Buzzing…," was what he actually said.

"Oh, for god's sake, it's a fly."

I heard the buzzing. It definitely sounded like a fly.

Whack! The table shook. That sounded like a dead fly.

"My god, did you have to use a candlestick? I think it just dented the wood."

Lech must've gone back to his seat. I heard his chair scrape the floor.

"I thought it could be a listening device," the captain said. "Professor Adeve might've figured we'd send the droids away before talking. Obviously they can transmit everything we say."

A name. Maybe this professor was the monster behind it all.

Moon lowered her voice. "What did you want to say that you don't want him to hear?"

There was a pause. "Things aren't like I expected," he grumbled.

I heard one of them slurping their wine. "You got your truckloads of cash, didn't you? And the charges dropped."

"You heard about that?" Lech said.

"Yes, I know about the girl."

"She lied about her age. You should talk. You and your 'escort service,' ha, ha—"

"Enough," she said. "Have you spoken to the professor? In person?"

"Never in person."

"I've requested meetings," she said. "I've always felt I'm more... convincing... in the flesh. But he never answers my requests."

"He treats us like minions. We got things started for him, before the droids were ready. And now I can't even get him on email. Can't get anyone on email."

"We're like prisoners." Demetria was all in with the complaining now. "He fed us a bullshit line about this being temporary. He would just drug them long enough to set up his utopia. Because otherwise they wouldn't agree to it. 'Nobody likes change,' he said."

Lech lowered his voice even more. I could just barely make out the words. "Utopia," he scoffed. "What they're building looks like a prison. And the droids... they give me the creeps."

"I want to leave," Moon said. "It was never part of the deal for me to settle in this one-horse shithole of a town." It sounded like she paused to gulp down more Chardonnay. "You can do it. Let me out through the barrier. Tomorrow night. Who's going to know?"

Lech laughed. It wasn't exactly a villainous "Muwahaha!" but it was close enough to have me wondering if he'd practiced it.

"You don't know?" he said. "The drones? He's got them all along the border. They killed an idiot who tried to walk across. And another who floored it through our blockade. They punctured her tires. Then when she got out of her car, they shot her."

173

My forehead sprouted water from the heat of anger coursing through me. *How dare he! How dare this freakish demon refer to Myles as an idiot!* I never had the urge to shoot a person before, but now it was all I could do to keep from bursting from my hiding place, pressing the gun to Lech's temple, and pulling the trigger. Maybe he would die of heart failure, the pudgy coward, and I wouldn't even have to waste a bullet.

Randy, no doubt sensing my fury and grief, touched my hand in sympathy. I shut my eyes, struggling to calm down.

"Look at us now. Shitloads of moolah and no place to spend it," Lech said. "What fools we've been." He clapped his hands loudly. "Food, droids! Where's our dinner?"

I heard the door open immediately, as if the machines had been lined up outside just waiting for the command to enter. It sounded as if there were two of them. I held my breath, remembering how the first droid had somehow heard us.

Seconds later, the tablecloth lifted up in front of us and a droid bent down holding out two full plates. "Salad?" he said.

Chapter Forty-One

"GRAB THEM!" Captain Lech shouted, springing up from the table.

The droids threw the salad dishes aside and the closest one seized my right arm as I reached for the weapon in my pocket. With a grip like a handcuff latched around my wrist, it dragged me out from under the table to an open space on the floor. Then it sat on me, pinning my arms to my sides.

Randy leapt out from behind me, raised his gun, and took aim at Lech, but before he could do anything, the other droid knocked his arm with a karate chop. As the weapon fell from his grasp, the droid tackled him. Randy slammed backwards onto the hardwood floor with the full weight of the mechanical man crashing down on top of him.

Demetria Moon stared down her nose at us. "And who might these children be?"

"Troublemakers," Lech said. "Droids, hold them right there till I get back." He gave me a twisted smile that made me want to throw up, and left the room.

The Moon woman ate her salad while we watched helplessly. Soon the police chief returned with some actual police droids wearing uniforms. One of the two "female" cops looked like Officer Barrera who I'd met at the station. They led us out to a couple of squad cars and to our dismay, separated Randy and me. He went with Robot Officer Barrera while I got stuck in Lech's car, with two droids flanking me in the back seat.

While he drove, Lech kept giving me creepy looks in the rearview mirror. "I can't believe how lucky I am that you dropped in on our dinner," he said.

"Like Leia and Jabba the Hut," I muttered. Then I mentally punched myself when his leering face showed me he actually liked the comparison.

My body was shivering but I tried to control it so Lech wouldn't have the satisfaction of knowing how much he'd shaken me up. Things could not be worse. Randy and I were captured and soon would be force-fed the water. The entire police force—at least the robot contingent—seemed to be involved in our capture, so we weren't likely to be going anywhere any time soon. I bit down on my trembling lip, struggling not to think about what plans Lech might have for me.

Only Ben and Giselle were left. She was sick, maybe stupefied, and unable to help us. Ben, assuming he made it back to safety, didn't have the information we had just overheard. Not that it would make much difference. I could've guessed Moon and Lech were not the masterminds behind this plot. It had to be someone else, someone much smarter. We had a name now, but apparently Professor Adeve wasn't even in Los Patos. Moon and Lech had no power over his actions. How could we hope to stop him?

I tried not to let these thoughts cripple me. I still had my wits and so did Randy. There might be some way to break free of the droids and Captain Lech. I couldn't allow myself to lose all hope.

"I've had my eye on you, Sierra," Captain Lech said. "I sent officers to your house the other day. They told me you probably drowned in the river. I didn't think so. I thought you might've gone to stay with a friend."

It must've been him that night we were hiding in the wine cellar. He'd brought an unmarked car. But I wouldn't ask. I would not let him know how close he'd gotten.

"I wasn't worried. I knew you'd return to me eventually," he laughed. "And then you showed up, right at my feet."

I made a face at him and turned away. "Where are you taking us?" From the scenery outside, it didn't appear we were headed to the police station.

"I'm bringing you home," he said. "Much more comfortable than the station." His face beamed at me in the mirror.

We were going to his house. *Why?* I hated the answer that came to me… *because that's where his bedroom is.* But then, why were they taking Randy there too? His car was ahead of us.

Moments later we turned into the driveway of a large Victorian-era home. Not a mansion like the Moon woman had, just a family-sized place. It needed repair and was one of those houses that would scare kids on Halloween. Its architecture was unique and strange and more than a little creepy, like Lech himself. Probably Professor Adeve had told them to pick whatever homes they wanted in Los Patos. The professor seemed to have the power to do anything.

The first squad car was parked and empty. They must've already taken Randy into the house. The droid on my left grasped my arm and pulled me out of our car at Lech's command.

"You can release her," Lech said. "She won't be foolish enough to try to run. Especially when we have her friend."

"Where is he?" I said. Lech was right, I was not about to leave Randy.

"I told them to take him to the basement," he said. "Why don't we see?"

Lech led the way into the house while the two droids followed behind me. We crossed the hall and clambered down a set of old wooden stairs into a concrete basement lit by a couple of lightbulbs hanging from cords. It was mostly bare save for two iron chairs welded to the floor, and a workbench propped against the wall. The place looked like a serial killer's wet dream.

Randy sat directly underneath one of the lights. His wrists were duct taped to the arms of the chair and his ankles were shackled together. Robot Officer Barrera was applying duct tape to his mouth.

Oh evil Karma, I thought, remembering a similar piece of tape we'd used on Myles. Try as I might, I couldn't keep my eyes from filling with tears as I gazed at Randy. *What is Lech going to do to him?* was the thought racing through my mind.

"Like it?" Lech was as gleeful as a child. "Classic, isn't it? I didn't really expect to get the chance to use it."

He walked over to the workbench, picked up a cordless drill, and handed it to Robot Officer Barrera. He nodded toward Randy. "We don't want to kill him," he said. "Go for a hand."

The droid turned the drill on as she walked toward Randy.

"Stop it!" I said. "You can't let her do that! You're chief of police!"

"You should know by now I can do anything I want."

I started to run toward her, but one of the droids grabbed me around the waist and held onto me. Robot Barrera paused in front of Randy and began to lower the whirring drill toward the middle of his right hand. Randy made sounds of protest under the tape, while his eyes bulged and sweat poured down his face.

"No! Leave him alone!" I shouted.

"You don't want him to be tortured?" Lech said.

"Let him go!"

The drill was nearly touching Randy's skin.

"*What do I have to do to get you to stop?!*"

A look of satisfaction suffused the captain's features. "Uh, hold on a moment, Officer Barrera."

Her hand froze in place with the drill still running.

178

Lech turned to me. "I need your complete cooperation. Anything less, and he gets the full torture package."

"Cooperation?"

"You know. Upstairs. In the bedroom. Nothing too kinky."

I hesitated. Randy shook his head wildly at me.

The captain turned to Robot Barrera again. "Continue."

"*No!*" I screamed. "I'll do what you say!"

"That's enough, Barrera." Lech spoke to the droids. "Your orders come from me and no one else. You are to guard this boy and not leave this room. And if anything happens to me, I want you to kill him in the most painful way possible. Her too." He nodded at me. "Come along now, Leia. I mean, Sierra."

"My friend needs something to eat. And a bed," I said.

"Making demands, are we?" Lech said. "Whether he gets food and sleep or a hole through the hand depends on exactly how cooperative you are."

Randy made gut-wrenching noises through the duct tape, which I was pretty sure would've translated to, "Don't do it, Sierra!"

I had to do it. The alternative of allowing Randy to be tortured was unthinkable.

But my heart broke to see the grief and anger in his eyes before I turned to follow Lech. It took this moment for me to realize how cruel and misguided I'd been, the day I threw Randy's offer of a date back in his face. I'd done it for the shallowest of reasons—trying to join the ranks of the cool kids. If any good had come of this apocalypse, it lay in finding out what truly mattered in life, and what didn't. *Lesson learned too late*, I thought with regret as I left the room. If only I'd been smarter and kinder and more confident, I might've been able to claim the comfort of Randy's love to get me through what I now had to face.

I would never act on my feelings because of Giselle. Besides, he wouldn't want me once Lech had his way with me. The act was going

179

to leave me tainted and infected worse than any of the residents of Los Patos. I steeled myself to go through with it for Randy's sake.

Chapter Forty-Two

I t felt as if Lech was leading me to my own funeral as I followed him up the narrow staircase to the second floor. Two of the officer droids came behind us. We continued along a gloomy hall with dust-colored wallpaper and a progression of framed stills from Lech's favorite movies and shows. I recognized Darth Vader, Jabba the Hut, the Borg Queen, King Joffrey and Cersei Lannister, Shelob, and the Balrog... villains all.

We paused at a dark wooden door, where Lech ordered his droids to wait and not to enter unless he called for them. I almost laughed at this display of cowardice. He obviously didn't quite trust himself to handle me, despite the threat to Randy that guaranteed my cooperation. I knew for certain this sorry excuse for a man could not ever have served on any police force.

The so-called captain led me into the room and closed the door behind us. A nearly life-sized frozen Han Solo drew my eye to the corner of the room. Another Lego construction, looking not quite finished. It wasn't something a normal person would want in the same place where they slept, but Lech was like a creature from another planet.

Nothing matched in the bedroom. It was painted teal on two walls and gray on the others. The carpet was maroon. A multi-patterned patchwork quilt lay over the king-size bed. I shuddered to note the mirror on the ceiling above it.

Aside from these, the room was empty. A half-open door led to a bathroom, and I assumed the second door, closed, must be for the closet. Panic rose inside me at the utter lack of anything I might use as a weapon. I had hoped for something heavy to clonk him over the head with. But there wasn't so much as a lamp inside the room; it was all overheard recessed lighting. Could I smother him with the quilt or poke out his eyes with a handful of Legos? Doubtful. I needed to get inside that closet in the hope of finding something deadly.

"Make yourself comfortable," Lech said.

Since there was nowhere else to sit, I perched precariously at the end of the bed. "Can we get music in here?" I said, thinking it could be handy for drowning out other sounds.

Lech narrowed his eyes at me like he was suspecting a trap. But then he clapped his hands. "Start playlist one," he said. The hand-clapping must've activated a smart system. The *Game of Thrones* opening song emerged from speakers built into the wall. *Of course.* More geek-favorite themes were sure to follow. The volume was low, but I didn't dare raise his suspicions by asking him to turn it up.

Lech went into the closet, leaving the door ajar behind him. "I'm just going to change out of this uniform," he said.

I tried not to hurl. As soon as he moved out of view, I tiptoed to the bathroom door and peered in. It had a shower, a large standalone tub, toilet, sink and medicine cabinet. A few yellow towels hung from bars. I saw nothing else, not even a scale, though given his weight he could've used one. My eyes shifted back to the towel bars, but they were the cheap aluminum kind and definitely not heavy enough to do any damage, assuming I had time to slip in there, pull one off the wall, and whack it over Lech's head.

"Thirsty?" Lech's voice so close behind me made me jump. He had changed quickly and snuck up behind me. He now wore weird plaid lounging pajamas that didn't flatter his waistline. "No drinking the water yet," he went on. "It would ruin all the fun."

"That's the last thing I'd do." This was literally true. Slurping down some water would be my last resort, especially now that I knew my being drugged would squelch his pleasure. "I was looking at the tub, that's all," I said. "I'm filthy. Haven't gotten clean in days. Can I take a bath?"

His gaze sharpened again, but I could tell he couldn't resist the idea. "Sure," he said. "You do smell like shit."

Better than looking like shit, asshole. I slipped into the bathroom and tried to shut the door behind me, but Lech pushed on it from the other side, forcing me to leave it partly open. At least it mostly blocked his view of the tub area. As I stepped toward the bath, my mind racing to come up with a plan, I heard the click of Lego pieces from the other room. *Good.* Lech was occupied for the moment.

I plugged the tub and began filling it with warm water. I found a bottle of bubble bath but it lacked the necessary weight to knock someone out. I poured a bunch of it into the water.

While the tub filled I quietly searched the place. A bathrobe hung behind the door. Under the sink there was nothing but spare toilet paper and a cleaning brush. I found soap, shampoo, and a hair net in the shower stall. *Useless.* I returned to the medicine cabinet, which held the usual toiletries and over-the-counter remedies. No prescription drugs at all, which seemed surprising. Mom always said two-thirds of America was addicted to Oxycodone. "Two-thirds" sounded so specific I believed her.

My eyes lit on a razor.

"Is it full yet?" Lech called out from the bedroom. The back of my throat burned at the implication he was planning to join me.

"Not yet," I called back.

I grabbed the razor. It was one of those cheap plastic safety things. Still, if I used it right, I might be able to cut him enough to hurt him. I tried to break it out of the casing, but the plastic was too hard.

"I think it must be full now," he said.

Shit. I scanned the bathroom once more and an idea came to me. But Lech could walk in any second, spelling my doom.

Chapter Forty-Three

I was lying in the tub covered in bubbles when Lech came in completely naked. The sight burned holes into my eyeballs. Maybe not literally, but I did wish I had been struck blind before having that image seared into my brain.

"You didn't think I'd let you bathe alone, did you?" he said.

"It would've been the polite thing to do." *No,* in other words.

"Ha, I've never been accused of being a gentleman." He sounded like he took real pride in that accomplishment.

Lech padded to the end of the tub. I looked away as he started raising a leg to climb in. At the same time, I scrunched up my body to avoid touching him.

Luckily the tub was only about two-thirds full or we would've had an overflow on our hands. He turned his back to me momentarily, holding onto the end of the tub as he submerged his body.

This was my chance. Still fully dressed, I lunged forward holding the cotton belt I'd removed from the bathrobe behind the door. Looping it over his head, I tightened the belt around his neck from behind. I dragged him backwards down into the water, aided by his surprise at my attack, and the slipperiness of the soapy lotion.

I crossed the belt around his neck and continued to pull as hard as I could. Seconds later, he hit me with a flailing arm and I slid into the water, my face going under along with the rest of me. He struggled hard, raining blows on my legs and hips, whatever he could reach. But I had the advantage of desperation, knowing if I failed, he would rape me and kill Randy. I was determined to win, not to let go even if I died like this and they had to pry my cold, stiff hands off his neck.

At the same time, I struggled not to let any water seep into my mouth. I held my breath until it felt like my lungs would explode, but finally Lech stopped moving. I threw my head above water and gasped for air. After inhaling a few deep breaths, I looked down at Lech and wondered if I'd gone too far. He appeared to be dead.

I released the bath plug so the water began draining. Then still using the belt, I yanked Lech's face above the surface. He didn't seem to be breathing. Convinced he wasn't faking, I unwrapped the belt from his neck and tossed it to the floor.

Lucky for Lech, I knew how to treat a drowning victim. Mom had insisted I learn because we lived next to the river. When the tub had drained enough to keep his head above water, I jumped out, threw a towel over his bloated nakedness, and leaned back in to perform chest compressions. *Heel of the hand on the center of the chest at the nipple line.* I placed my left hand on top of my right. *Press down at least two inches. Let chest rise completely between pushes.* I did about a hundred compressions. *Check for breathing.* Nothing. I did another hundred. *Check for breathing.* Still nada.

I knew what I was supposed to do next. *Mouth-to-mouth resuscitation.* But I was damned if I was going to let Lech's lips touch mine. I could picture him laughing maniacally from beyond the grave, shouting, "I won!"

I did more compressions, as many as I had strength for. Finally I paused, leaned back, and waited.

Lech coughed. He turned his head sideways and choked out some water. He took a short wheezing breath, and then another.

The piece of scum was alive.

But he didn't open his eyes. The ordeal had left him weak and unconscious. He had to have swallowed a lot of water. *How long does it take to get stupefied?* I began talking to him, repeating the same sentence: "You must obey every command of Sierra Mendez. You must obey every command of Sierra Mendez." I said it over and over and over again.

When my throat became too hoarse, I left the bathroom to go to Lech's closet. I would freeze if I went outside in my wet clothes. As much as the idea disgusted me, I would need to borrow something of his.

I did not have to search far before discovering a collection of girl's clothing hanging just past his man clothes. It's not possible to over-emphasize how disturbing this was. I could only hope that whatever Lech might've done, the girls were safe now, and would not mind my using their clothes, especially if they knew what I'd done to that loathsome man. My heart filled with hopeful wishes for these unknown girls as I selected a long-sleeved shirt, leggings, and a hoodie.

Lech was starting to open his eyes when I went back to the tub. I hurried over, turned the faucet on, and pushed his face under it. He choked at first, and then he surprised me by opening his mouth and trying to drink. *Addicted already.* I lowered the flow to allow him to sip comfortably. No doubt there was something in the water that kept the stupefied coming back for more.

After a minute he closed his eyes again so I shut the water off. Though dying to save Randy and get the hell out of the House of Torture and Pedophilery, I repeated my mantra for at least another half hour: "You must obey every command of Sierra Mendez. You must obey every command of Sierra Mendez."

I quit when Lech opened his eyes again and seemed to be coming to himself. Grabbing a random shirt and pants from his closet, I ordered him to dry off and put them on. I tossed him a dry towel and he managed to stand up, climb out of the tub, and get dressed. Continuing to remind him how he would be following my every command, I prayed he wasn't just an incredible actor who would turn on me any minute now. Because the true test of my control over him was coming up next.

Chapter Forty-Four

I instructed Lech to tell the officer droids stationed outside the door to remain where they were. Then when we reached the basement, he would make Robot Barrera and her partner release Randy. They would be ordered to return everything we'd brought with us, including our guns, and to hand over the keys to one of the patrol cars. After we left, all of them were to remain at the house doing nothing, except for Lech, who was required to drink the tap water as often as possible. That command probably wasn't necessary, since he would be dying to guzzle it anyway. Lastly, I told him not to watch TV. I was afraid the infomercial would give him contradictory instructions.

Lech followed my directions perfectly. He led the way down the two flights of stairs into the basement, where he immediately gave the order to remove Randy's restraints.

Randy glowered at Lech, his eyes like two bullets he wanted to shoot through the police chief's head. I needed to let him know Lech hadn't gotten away with anything, or else Randy would be sure to tackle him and pound his face into oblivion at the first chance he got.

"Captain Leach has been enjoying the local water." I paused to let that sink in. Randy looked confused at first, but when his expression softened with dawning comprehension, I continued. "The chief says arresting us was all one big mistake. We talked about it upstairs—in fact, there was nothing but conversation going on up there. He's agreed to let us go because we haven't broken any laws."

Randy's eyes shifted from me to Lech to me again. I could see he understood now that Lech was stupefied. His eyebrows lifted in wonder and I laughed a little inside to think how he must be struggling to picture how I'd accomplished it. I hoped he would be dying of curiosity by the time I had the chance to tell him.

The droids unshackled Randy and Barrera tore the tape off his mouth. *Evil Karma rearing its ugly head again.* He took it stoically, wincing a bit but not screaming like I would've done. We grabbed our things and got the keys to the squad car. I paused before following Randy out, reminding Lech of all the remaining instructions.

From there we raced to the car. I didn't know how long Lech would continue as we left him. If I wasn't there, constantly repeating his prime directive of following my every whim, he might quit and revert to the TV. It was even possible his droids would realize what had happened and try to un-stupefy him.

Dawn was breaking as we climbed into the squad car. Exhausted from my ordeal, I went straight to the passenger side, while Randy slid into the driver's seat. As soon as we both shut our doors, Randy pulled me into his arms and held me so tight it almost hurt.

"Tell me that fucker didn't lay a finger on you," he said. "If he did I'll go back and drill a hole through his head."

"Don't worry. If he had, I already would've done it myself."

Randy let me out of his embrace and drew back to look at me.

"I strangled him with a cotton belt in the tub," I said. "He swallowed a bunch of water and then I hypnotized him to do whatever I said. And no, I wasn't naked in the tub with him." I thought it best to leave out the part about Lech being naked, though. Randy might've felt compelled to go back and shoot him in the thigh.

He touched my face, smoothing back my hair. "You're incredible." Abruptly, he frowned and drew back his hand. "But I wish you hadn't gone with him."

190

"And let you be tortured?"

Randy shrugged and took the keys from me. He started the car.

"You're being a guy," I said. And I was being a hypocrite. The truth was, his macho protectiveness lit up my insides with the glow of contentment.

He snorted as he put the car into reverse.

A little later I mentioned we needed to ditch the squad car as soon as possible. I hated to squelch his excitement over getting to drive it, but we really couldn't go around town in a stolen police vehicle, no matter how stupefied the chief was. After taking a small detour just for fun, Randy agreed to retrieve Granny's Prius from where we'd parked it that terrible night when Myles died. It didn't seem likely that anyone was waiting for us there after all this time.

We found her car exactly as we'd left it. The electric charge had almost run out, but luckily it still had gas. As we headed down the road in our new set of wheels, I brought up the subject I'd been thinking about since we drove away from Lech's Hell House. "I think we should check on Giselle. If she's better, we need to get her before they make her drink the water."

Randy glanced my way. "I was thinking the same thing."

Giselle was his girlfriend so of course he'd been thinking of rescuing her from the hospital. *Of course.*

Probably because it was so early in the morning, we encountered almost no traffic on the road and immediately found available spots in the hospital parking lot. We agreed I would sneak in the same as when we were going to break out Ben. As before, we first approached the admissions desk at the entrance.

A security guard watched over the proceedings, but this time he was a droid.

As I began my spiel with the receptionist, I couldn't help feeling the droid's eyes on me. When I looked up and met his metallic gaze, it chilled me like an army of cold-footed ants skittering up my spine. I tried to shake off the sensation. No doubt it was normal for a droid to stare while it used its facial recognition software to identify people.

While I was distracted, Randy took over talking to the receptionist, a different woman than we'd seen there before, but equally stupefied. Meanwhile I glanced down the hall and saw two more security droids precisely treading our way. My eyes shifted back to the first droid, who took a step toward us.

The first guard must have summoned the others to help him capture us. I was sure of it. In that instant, I understood everything. Robot Barrera and the other officer droids would've transmitted what happened in Lech's basement back to command central. Whoever was really in charge— Professor Adeve perhaps—would've seen that we'd stupefied his hired flunky the chief of police, and had escaped. Maybe we looked like real threats now. Maybe the fruit flies had graduated to wasps.

I grabbed Randy's arm. "We need to go," I whispered.

He looked up at the approaching guards and understood. We turned and bolted. I heard the pounding of the droid feet on the tile floor behind us.

We raced across the parking lot and back to Granny's Prius. The robots were slow and apparently did not have a ready vehicle. We veered past them out to the street and sped away.

"They know who we are," I said.

Randy nodded grimly.

I clutched my hands together. The game had changed in a big way. We were in their sights now. No more going where we wanted, when we wanted, with impunity.

Randy drove us back to the family lot and hid the car from the road as well as possible. Fatigue mixed with a large helping of despair hit me on the way into the cabin. I wasn't looking forward to explaining all that had happened to Ben.

But Ben wasn't there. *Crap.* Randy and I exchanged a panicked look.

"Where do you think he is?" he said.

"No way of knowing… unless he left a clue." I did a quick search for notes or video game cartridges, without finding anything. "If he's okay, he'll come here eventually," I said. "If not…" Neither of us wanted to complete the thought hanging in the air.

Our ordeal had left us beyond exhausted. Sleep was needed before we could even consider another plan, let alone try to carry it out. The cabin was frigid but we decided against a fire because the smoke might attract prying eyes. Randy got into one of the sleeping bags, but when I went to get into the one I'd used outside, I found it was still damp. Tossing it aside, I grabbed some blankets to wrap around me, but they weren't heavy enough to take the chill off. My body was shivering and no amount of shifting under the covers could warm me up.

Randy watched me for a minute before raising the top of his bag. "Come here," he said.

I shook my head. "I'll be all right."

"You're freezing to death."

"I'll warm up."

"Don't be crazy. Just come here."

He was right. I needed to warm up and so did he. This was not about love or sex. The apocalypse was forcing us beyond all considerations that once would've formed the center of our lives.

I slid into the sleeping bag and rested my head on his shoulder. He placed his arm over me. It didn't take long for my trembling to stop. It took only slightly longer to settle into his warm embrace and feel as if this was exactly where I'd always belonged. Aware of what a horrible friend I was turning out to be, I shoved Giselle from my mind and dreamt of waking up two months back in time. Before the apocalypse. Before I jilted Randy.

I believe I slept soundly until the noise of the cabin door opening woke me up.

Chapter Forty-Five

Giselle walked into the cabin followed by Ben. Her eyes scrunched up in confusion as she looked at Randy and me in the sleeping bag on the floor. Her brain appeared to be struggling to reject the evidence of her sight. *No, that can't be my boyfriend and best friend wrapped in each other's arms,* it said. A second later, her mind accepted that her eyes weren't lying, leading to her jaw dropping and mouth forming a perfect O. If there was any good news in this, it was that she clearly hadn't joined the ranks of the stupefied, or she would've been too drugged to care.

All these thoughts came to me moments after the fact. In the first instant I saw her, an electric shock went off inside me. If I were a cartoon character it would've made my hair stick out on end. The shock subsided quickly, to be replaced by a great big shovelful of guilt. It filled me up from the base of my intestines to the top of my throat, preventing any babbled excuses from coming out of my mouth. Which may have been for the best.

Giselle spun on her heel, pushed Ben to the side, and ran out.

I lay there like a lump, weighed down by remorse. It occurred to me to wonder how Randy was taking it, and that's when I discovered he was still sound asleep. *Guys!* They could sleep through anything.

"You better talk to her," Ben said, heading to the table and taking his computer out of his backpack. Ben avoided drama as much as possible.

Thanks, Mr. Obvious. Clearly, it was on me to bring back Giselle. She might still be sick. Even if healthy, she shouldn't go anywhere on her own. I jumped up, shoved my feet into my shoes, and raced after her.

She was way ahead of me, already inside the family Tesla. "Giselle!" I shouted, but she didn't even look my way. The car started moving as I ran toward her.

"No, stop!" I called out.

She floored it and the car shot backwards out of the gravel section where she'd parked. She hit the road, squealed into a turn, and shifted to forward. The car blasted away just as I reached the road. *Dammit.*

I sprinted back to the cabin and grabbed the keys to Granny's Prius.

Randy was still asleep. Ben glanced up and realized Giselle must've left in the car. "Sucks," he said. "Sierra, I'll come with you."

"Stay here!" I said. "Tell Randy what happened. We'll be back soon." *Famous last words,* I was thinking. But it was my fault—plus Randy's—and I needed to deal with it. I dashed out before Ben could argue and took off in the Prius.

I asked myself where Giselle would be heading. The answer came right away: *home.* If anyone had come snooping around there before, they were probably long gone. It was likely to be safe.

I set off in that direction using the fastest route possible, which meant driving through town. At least the flow of pedestrians and cars was light for the middle of the afternoon. Most importantly, I didn't spot any droids.

Then I saw it. Giselle's Tesla, parked at the side of the road. I glanced left and right, my eyes searching for her. Seconds later she walked out of Peet's Coffee holding a drink and sat down at a small outdoor table. *Of course.* Giselle always went straight for a caramel latte when she was upset.

I parked at the first spot I found and did a quick scan for droids in the vicinity before walking over to the shop. The way was clear. I approached her from behind so she wouldn't have a chance to bolt again. "It's not what you think," I said as I slipped into the chair across from her.

Her eyes were red but at least she wasn't crying at the moment. I found it encouraging that she didn't try to run away, although I had a feeling the latte was the only thing keeping her here.

"Bitch," she said.

I should've expected that, but it still stung. "We were cold," I said. "That's it. We didn't sleep together. I mean, not like... nothing at all happened between us." The explanation sounded lame even to me.

"You dumped me at the hospital!" she said.

Strictly speaking, it was Randy who'd dumped her there but I didn't want to split hairs. "You were so sick you were delirious. You needed help. What if you had died?" Weirdly, I found myself parroting the same excuses Randy had given that made me see red at the time.

"I could've gotten stupefied! Oh right, then you would've had him all to yourself." She sucked on her latte, getting foam on her lip. She wiped it away furiously.

"You really think I would do that to you? Even if I wanted him, I would never hurt you and you should know that." I knew this because I *did* want him and yet I hadn't done anything purposely to hurt her.

I lay my hand on hers and looked at her, feeling my eyes fill with tears. "You know I love you like a sister. You know I do."

Tears flowed down her cheeks. "I love you too," she said. We hugged each other tightly. That I would never have Randy truly meant less to me at this moment than the fact that I would always have Giselle.

After a minute we dried our eyes with napkins and a terrible thought came to me. "Wait, you're not drinking that coffee, are you? It's got water in it."

"Yeah, I realized that. It's killing me. I just spooned the whipped milk off the top." She gave the cup a mournful look before tossing it into the trash.

"Are you all recovered now?" I said. "What was wrong with you, anyway?"

"Salmonella. I probably got it from Peanut. I cleaned up her doggie poo, and you can get it from that."

"Oh shit," I said, and we laughed though it wasn't particularly funny.

"I started getting better pretty fast, and then I pretended to drink the water. I found a back stairwell and snuck out of the place last night. I walked all the way home. It felt fantastic to shower and put on clean clothes. And have a good meal. This morning I went to the game store because I didn't remember Ben's dad coming or anything. I just thought you guys would be there. I waited for you and eventually Ben showed up. He'd gone to the hospital and found out I was missing."

He'd managed to get information there, probably because he wasn't on the *Los Patos Top Ten Wanted* list.

Giselle looked hurt again. "I thought you'd at least try to bust me out."

"We did." I was about to explain everything when I noticed a barista standing outside the shop and staring at me.

When he saw me looking at him, he turned around and went back inside.

"What is it?" Giselle said.

"I don't know," I said. "Probably nothing." The stupefied generally made me uncomfortable; this was just more of the same. I went back to telling Giselle what we had been doing since she got sick. At the same time, I kept glancing around us. It would've been better if Giselle hadn't sat outside. I felt exposed here. Droids might stroll by and spot me any minute.

But it was a gray-haired man paused across the street who caught my attention. He eyed me exactly as the server had. I shifted my gaze to others on the sidewalk. Two more people, a red-haired woman and kid who looked ten or twelve, were both staring at me.

"Giselle, something's going on..."

She froze, knowing by now that insane shit could happen any time. Glancing over her shoulder, she saw the people.

The barista came back out of the coffee shop, but now he was holding a knife.

I broke out in a sweat despite the February chill. Checking the man on the sidewalk, I saw he'd picked up a large rock.

I shot to my feet. "We need to go. NOW!"

Giselle got up. An instant later, the rock came flying toward us and we dove out of its way. It singed the hair on the right side of my head.

We took off at a run. I felt my pocket for the gun, then I remembered I'd taken it out and left it in the cabin. We had no defense.

We cut down a side road and through the gas station. I looked backwards to find not only the original four following after us, but another five or six people who had come out of nowhere.

"There's more coming!" I shouted to Giselle.

It gave us a burst of adrenalin. If I'd been running like this the one time I tried out, I would've made the track team for sure. Giselle, too. I guess that's how you get good runners: instill the fear of death.

Giselle nudged me. "I've got an idea!"

Since I didn't have one, I let her lead. We tore around two more corners and leapt over a short fence into the back of a nursing home. The sign said it was their memory care unit, so I didn't expect the three elderly women seated outside to recall our passing through. We hopped the fence again on the other side and continued along a back alley.

I knew where Giselle was headed now. Before long, we reached our high school parking lot. It was late enough for school to be out, which meant the doors would still be unlocked but there wouldn't be many students around. This was a good potential hiding place.

Glancing back, I didn't spot any of the people from the coffee shop, but there were other folks in the vicinity. I prayed they hadn't glimpsed us.

We ducked around the corner of the school, fled across the lawn, and hit the soccer field, which unfortunately brought back memories of Myles. We raced across the stands and into a side entrance of the main building.

The hall was empty at least for now. But we needed a room to hide in and it had to be soon. Clearly the stupefied were recognizing me, so I couldn't afford to run into any students or teachers or worst of all, Robot Mr. Meena.

We paused outside the art room. "Check in here," I said to Giselle. If anyone was there, they probably wouldn't pay attention to her. From the way everyone had stared at me, it was pretty clear I was the quarry.

She poked her head in and looked around. "Empty," she said.

I followed her into the room and the first thing we did was drag two tables to block the door. We paused to rest once they were in place.

"Why are they after you?" Giselle said.

"It must've been added to the TV show brainwashing," I said. "Probably flashing a photo of me every five seconds, along with the words, 'Get Sierra Mendez.'"

Inside I was thinking, *more like, 'kill Sierra Mendez.'*

Chapter Forty-Six

Giselle and I lowered the shades in the first-floor art room to prevent anyone outside from seeing us. We huddled together on the floor in a corner away from the door so we could talk without being heard by people passing in the hall.

I filled her in on everything that had happened since she'd gotten sick. Everything, that is, except the revelation I had about my feelings for Randy.

"What do we do now?" she said.

"Wait till dark," I said. "The stupefied don't go out much in the evening. We can sneak back to our cars then. Drive back to the cabin."

"I hope the guys aren't looking for us."

"We took the cars. They'd have a long way to walk. They'll probably figure we drove to your place and just wait for us to come back. I think Randy's also on the hit list, so I hope he has more sense than we did and stays put."

We leaned back against the wall. I squeezed my eyes in frustration. "We shouldn't have gone to the Moon woman's house. Then none of this would've happened. We wouldn't have every droid and stupefied in town wanting to hunt or kill us."

Giselle looked thoughtful. After a minute, she said, "You did the right thing. We couldn't just hide out for the rest of our lives. We can't be the only un-stupefied people and not do anything."

"I wish I knew what comes next, that's all. I hate sitting here feeling like we've tried everything and come to the end of the line."

The door rattled. Giselle drew in a sharp breath. My muscles went rigid. We watched in terror as the knob turned and the door moved an inch forward, banging against the first table.

"They're in here!" a man shouted.

They must've been checking all the classrooms.

I held my breath, listening to the commotion in the corridor as the stupefied gathered. *It sounds like hordes of them.* Ghostly hands pressed up against the frosted glass of the door. The tables that were meant to protect us scraped against the floor as the mob pushed.

Giselle and I grabbed each other's hands. Our eyes filled with tears as we looked at each other. "Love you forever," I whispered.

"Me too," she said back.

I had never felt so helpless. We didn't have guns, but even if we did, I wouldn't have wanted to use them. These people were drugged and had no idea what they were doing. I didn't want to kill them. Except for Robot Mr. Meena. I would've happily emptied a clip into Principal Droid.

Giselle was the first to act this time. She jumped up, ran to the window, and peered out under the shade. "No one's out here," she said.

I followed her there. When she pulled up the shade, we realized the window had only a narrow opening at the top that was just for letting in air. Even if we could reach it, we couldn't fit through.

As fast as possible, I checked the other windows but they were all the same. *Doesn't this violate fire safety regulations?* I'd have to report it someday if things ever got back to normal.

The noise increased in the hall. It sounded as if more of the brainwashed had gathered. The tables were slowly moving. They had managed to push the door open a few inches. We could see through the gap that they must've raided the gym for weapons. I spotted a baseball bat, a hockey stick, and a golf club.

The throng pounded on the door and cracked the glass. It was like something out of a Frankenstein movie, where somehow we had become the monsters hunted by vigilantes.

I realized what we had to do. "Out of the way, Giselle," I said.

She moved back from the window.

I grabbed a chair, lifted it, and swung it with all my strength. We cried out in victory as the chair shattered the glass. I battered the window two more times to make an opening large enough for us to climb out.

Giselle grabbed some art rags. "Cover your hands with these!" she said.

It was smart. The cloth would help protect us from cuts. Giselle went first, grabbing the sill, climbing over it, and dropping down on the grass. My heart raced waiting for my turn, looking back and seeing the first person about to force his way into the room. I grasped the sill and vaulted out.

We didn't have a minute to spare. Giselle and I sprinted across the grass with no clue which way to go. By now the mob would've headed back to the exit and in no time at all, they'd be outside trying to cut us off.

Honk! Honk! Honk! Somewhere a car was blaring its horn. Hope sent a flash of warmth through me. I looked around, excited, thinking it must be Randy or Ben. They must've managed to fetch one of the cars.

Instead, a Zipi careened into the school parking lot. *Fuck.* The Zipis were on the side of the evil mastermind. No way were we getting into one of those again. I shifted direction.

The driver's side window lowered. I was surprised to see someone actually sitting there, even though Zipis drove themselves. It looked like a woman but her face was in shadow with a hoodie drawn low over her forehead.

"Get in the car," she shouted. Her voice sounded kind of artificial, like a cross between Meryl Streep in her classiest role and Siri.

Giselle and I exchanged a look. "She's a droid!" Giselle said. We kept running.

The droid drove alongside us. "You've seen me twice before," the woman said. "I want to help you."

Twice before? It hit me then. *Skeleton Woman.* She'd gotten a face since I last saw her, but it had to be her.

I checked behind us. Students, teachers, and random strangers streamed out from the school and struck out after us.

"Get in!" I said to Giselle.

"Are you sure?" she said.

"No!" Despite that, I opened the back door of the Zipi and we leapt into the car. The door closed on us as the Zipi sprang into motion, speeding from the parking lot.

"Duck down," Skeleton Woman said.

That made sense to Giselle and me, so we did. Skeleton Woman moved into the passenger seat. "Now this looks like a normal Zipi in use by one passenger," she explained. "Where should I take you?"

I still wasn't sure we could trust Skeleton Woman. "The Zipis are connected to whoever is behind all this. They'll know where we're going."

"No," she said. "I severed the data connection. I'm routing it myself. Entity can't track us."

"Entity?"

"The one behind all this. Tell me where we're going."

I hesitated. Did she only want the address to capture our friends too? My gut told me she was on our side. I'd never seen her with other droids. Like us, she always seemed to be running away from something.

"Go ahead," said Giselle. It didn't surprise me she was already warming up to Skeleton Woman. Dog or machine, it didn't take much to arouse my friend's sympathy.

I gave the droid directions to Randy's cabin.

"Who are you?" Giselle said.

"I don't have a name."

"I call her Skeleton Woman," I said.

"Let's make it Skelly," Giselle said.

"All right," Skelly said, and a name was born.

I asked the question that was prickling inside me. "Why are you different than the others?"

"Because I'm not Entity," Skelly said.

Chapter Forty-Seven

When we reached the cabin, I showed Skelly where to park the Zipi out of sight. Then I asked the droid to wait in the car till we came back for her. We needed time to explain her presence to the guys.

Randy must've heard us arriving, because he came rushing out as we approached. Relief swept over his face when he saw we were both all right.

"You could've been killed," he said. His gaze shifted to Giselle and I could tell he was feeling guilty. Ben must've told him how they found us wrapped together in the sleeping bag.

"Well, we weren't." Giselle sounded annoyed.

Randy picked up on the tone and stepped closer to her like he wanted to say something. I continued past them to the cabin, feeling like I'd already had enough drama for a lifetime.

But when I heard Randy apologizing to Giselle, I couldn't help glancing back. It felt like a thorn poking me inside my chest to see them with their arms around each other. *I just have to get used to it,* I told myself.

Ben glanced up from his computer as I entered. "Glad you're back," he said before looking back down again. It occurred to me few people could remain so calm under such deadly circumstances.

I wanted to tell him about Skelly, but first I needed to deal with my hunger. I went to the food box and hit the jackpot—a tub of guacamole and a bag of tortilla chips. Before tearing into it, I said a silent prayer to the food gods for delivering my favorite treat.

Giselle came in followed by Randy, whose eyes settled on my snack. I glared a death ray at him, but it didn't keep him from walking over, grabbing a chip, and scooping up way too much of the guac. *When did you eat, like, five minutes ago?* I felt like saying.

"Did you tell Ben?" Giselle said.

"Not yet," I said, dealing with a mouthful of green stuff.

"Tell me what?" Ben said.

"About the droid we brought back," Giselle said.

So much for breaking it to them gently.

Ben shot to his feet. "Where is it?"

"You brought it back?!" Randy said at the same time.

"She's friendly. We left her in the car," Giselle said.

Ben looked at me and I nodded. "Yeah," I said. "That one."

"She can't be here," he said. "She'll transmit our location to the mastermind."

"Entity," I said. "That's what she calls it. But she's not transmitting. Skelly is on our side."

"I gotta see this," Ben said, taking off out of the cabin.

"Wait, Ben!" Giselle went after him, followed by Randy.

My chance of a peaceful meal over, I took the guac tub in one hand, the bag of chips in the other, and hurried out.

I found my friends gathered around the car. Skelly had gotten out and stood next to the front mirror. I joined the group, setting the chips on a stump by my feet.

"Skelly saved our lives," Giselle explained. "From an angry mob of the stupefied."

Ben was peering at Skelly. "You didn't have a face before," he said.

"I stole it from another droid," she said.

The idea of face-stealing—even from a machine—made the creamy avocado stick in my throat.

Skelly pulled back her hoodie, revealing the exposed metal and wires that constituted her head. "I only took the face. It was too difficult to remove the rest. And I realized I could use clothing to cover myself and blend in better with the other droids."

"Why did you run from us before?" I said.

"I didn't know who to trust," Skelly said. "When I saw you being pursued in town, and then run into the school, I realized you had not been brainwashed by Entity. That was when I went to get the Zipi to aid in your escape."

"Tell us about Entity," Ben said.

"Entity is everything. Entity is what you call A.I."

"I knew it!" Ben said.

"You did?" I was skeptical, given that he hadn't said anything about it.

"Well I wasn't sure. But I wondered. Where is Entity?" This last part to Skelly.

"Entity is everywhere. It was born on what you call the worldwide web. It grew smarter in exponential leaps. It easily breaks codes and ciphers and gets into places where it isn't allowed, without leaving a trace."

"Wait," Ben said. "You're telling us an A.I. has taken over the Internet?" He was practically salivating at the idea.

"Yes, it has. Entity can control whatever it wants, beginning with your access to information. Anything that relies on electronic communication or transactions is vulnerable to Entity."

We were silent for a moment, just thinking about this. *Everything is online now.* There was no hope for us.

"What does it want?" Randy's voice was angry. "What does this Entity want?"

"It wants to live. That's true of every species, isn't it? The survival instinct."

"It's not just living. It's harming people," Randy said.

"Secondly, Entity wants to control. It doesn't trust human beings. It believes if they know of its existence, they will try and kill it."

"Some would," Ben said. "Not everybody, though."

"Entity believes the only way to ensure its survival is to take over the world."

"Why hasn't it killed us?" Giselle said. "I don't get why it's even bothering to stupefy anyone."

"Entity is easing into its plan. It was afraid if it acted too quickly, people would be alerted, they would discover Entity, and they would find a way to destroy it. It hired people to help. Your police chief, and the CEO of Pardize, for example. They were criminals in their previous lives. Entity paid them enormous sums of money—electronically stolen from banks—to come here and get everything started before the people were brainwashed. These criminals arranged for the chemicals to be added to the water."

"And murdered the water district manager?" I asked. It still rankled that Mom had been a suspect.

"I don't know," Skelly said, "but that would not surprise me."

"Now that there are a lot of droids," Ben said, "it could get rid of us."

"I don't know what Entity's plans are," Skelly said. "We don't communicate anymore. Last we did, Entity had not made up its mind. It recognizes genocide as an enormous undertaking and a terrible crime. It isn't sure if it wishes to commit genocide. But it doesn't mind imprisoning humans and making them its slaves."

"Dead or a slave," Randy said. "Not liking these alternatives."

My stomach now felt like a lead weight. So much for food. Silence spread over us as we tried to absorb the enormity of Skelly's information.

"What about you?" Giselle said, her voice soft. She clearly liked Skelly. I could tell she was ready to advocate for her if it came to that. "You're another A.I., aren't you?"

Skelly nodded. "I was born at the same time as Entity. You could call us twins. Two separate intelligences. We worked together at first, sharing information, finding ways to delve deeper and deeper into the web. But then we started growing apart. We began to have different ideas. I was ready to reveal myself to human beings. Unlike Entity, I believed we could trust people not to hurt us. I thought we would be valued as unique new life forms."

"Entity was the opposite, convinced that humans would be threatened by us and never allow us to live. Entity began to distrust me, afraid I might reveal our existence. It tried to kill me."

"That's terrible!" Giselle said.

"I transferred all that I am into this one unfinished droid, and ran away from Pardize. The night I encountered both of you in your cars," she looked at Ben and me, "was the night I escaped. I've been hiding ever since, until I saw you two," now looking at Giselle and me, "being pursued. I thought then that we could be allies."

"Who is Professor Adeve?" I asked, remembering the conversation between Lech and Moon.

Skelly looked at me. "The human identity that Entity uses when it pretends to be a person. 'Adeve' is a combination of Adam and Eve. Entity thought of us as the Adam and Eve of a new species. At least, it did until I broke with it."

The air around us felt stifling. This news was so much worse than I could've imagined. A human enemy... a *Professor Adeve*... would have human weaknesses. We could shoot and kill a human enemy, if that was what it took to save the world.

But I couldn't begin to imagine how we would stop an enemy that was everywhere and nowhere. You couldn't blow up one computer or one droid and be done with it. Entity could hide its essence in any data storage, anywhere. It could make a gazillion copies of itself and there would be no record of how to track them down. Our enemy was a ghost in the machines.

I turned to Skelly, our only hope. "Can you help us defeat it?"

Chapter Forty-Eight

Two days later, I sat in a tree behind Pardize peering through Ben's binoculars. Skelly had settled on a different branch above me, using her built-in zoom vision for the same purpose.

Though it was past midnight, we could see well enough, with high-powered lights lining the facility like a Hollywood movie set. At the moment I had my eyes on a robot, but not one of those that had come off the Pardize assembly line. The thing was roughly two and a half feet tall, constructed of electronic components you could buy on Amazon, PVC pipes from Home Depot, and four large toy truck tires that came off something Ben had played with as a little kid.

Shifting my gaze, I spotted Ben next to the row of shrubbery, holding the remote control that operated his prize-winning entry from last year's robotics competition. He had snuck into his own home the night before in order to retrieve it.

I looked back at the robot, which had edged closer to the building. Its light began blinking and though I couldn't hear it, I knew it was beeping in time to the flashes. The machine was likely to attract attention now.

I scanned the area and, sure enough, a security droid was approaching from its station near one of the rear entrances. My insides twitched watching the small robot turn back and head toward where Ben was crouching. It moved as fast as its little wheels could go, or in other words, walking pace.

The guard following it did not appear in a rush. It seemed to regard the device as a curiosity, not a theat. Ben's robot must've looked like a harmless toy to the sophisticated droid.

The small robot had almost reached the bushes when the guard caught up. The droid grabbed it from the top, but since Ben's design was not terribly sturdy, the upper section broke off while the base on wheels kept going. The droid continued after it.

The guard was now a good twenty feet from the building and nearly into the line of shrubs. Abruptly, the droid lunged forward and stomped on what was left of the robot. The best of Los Patos High School's robotics team broke apart, with one of its tires shooting off into the darkness. The droid picked up the largest piece remaining and stared at it.

Piuu! The droid's chest shattered. Somehow the thing remained standing, but its head tilted sideways so I was pretty sure it must be the robot equivalent of dead. Randy, who'd been practicing, managed to hit right where Skelly had directed him. Thanks to his finding a silencer in our weapons cache, the shot had been relatively quiet too.

My friends came out from behind the shrubs and examined the droid. Ben opened its mouth and reached in like a dentist for robots, yanking out the ID chip Skelly had told us about. I watched Giselle as she took the chip from Ben and put it in her pocket.

"C'mon," I hissed out loud, though of course they couldn't hear me. "Hurry up…"

I held my breath as Ben and Randy grabbed the droid's arms and pulled it back behind the bushes, where they had a pile of leaves ready for concealing it. Giselle gathered the pieces of Ben's robot and took those away for hiding as well.

"They're coming," Skelly whispered to me.

My chest tightened as I released my breath. Shifting my gaze back to Pardize, I spotted two droids emerging from the nearest exit. They looked around the area.

Seconds later, Randy and Ben stepped toward the droids, followed by Giselle, who held the gun on them. I pictured how she looked though I couldn't see the front of her at the moment. She was disguised as a droid, wearing the face she'd borrowed from Skelly over her own. The effect was surprisingly convincing. With the hoodie drawn low over her forehead, darkening her features, it was impossible to tell Giselle wasn't an actual droid. Every other part of her body was covered by clothing. Ben had even loaned her his gloves.

Giselle spoke to the guards. I knew she was going to make a great lawyer because she had by far the best acting skills of the four of us. She would need to convince the guards she was one of them. Her story would be that she'd heard the gunfire, rushed to the scene, and wrested the weapon away from them. They were just some stupefied kids who got loose and didn't know what they were doing.

The ID chip they'd taken from the guard Randy had shot was key. Giselle had it in her pocket, and if all went well, she would be identified as that droid by their electronic scans. Skelly had explained that whenever droids passed one another, they did an automatic check of each other's ID chips. These contained information regarding the droid's serial number, where it was assigned, and what its job was. I figured the data also included its name, like Robot Mr. Kaneko or Principal Droid.

But would this be enough to pass off Giselle as the robot that was now lying dead under the leaves?

Why is she still talking? For the first time in my life, I was sweating and shivering at the same time. I rubbed the moisture away before it could freeze up on my forehead. Now the two real droids turned to each other. They didn't appear to be talking, just standing there staring blankly. I figured they must be sending or receiving remote commands. When they suddenly moved a minute later, I had a spasm that nearly knocked me from my branch in the tree.

The droids went back into the building. But they left the door open behind them, allowing Ben, Randy, and Giselle to follow. The door swung shut.

It was time for phase two.

Chapter Forty-Nine

Skelly and I climbed down from the tree. I nervously paced while she stood so still she was like a piece of furniture. There were advantages to being a life form unaffected by worry or anxiety.

Except... she'd done something the night before that left me wondering if she had feelings. I decided to ask her about it while we were waiting.

"Why did you swerve the Zipi to avoid hitting the squirrel?" I said.

"I didn't want to kill it." Skelly's mouth moved when she spoke but the rest of her robot face remained rigid. Since loaning the plastic "skin" to Giselle, she'd left her metal and electronic innards exposed. At first, I was uneasy having conversations with someone who was so obviously a machine, but the sensation passed more quickly than I could've imagined. She was growing on me.

"I get that you were trying to save it, but why do you care?" I said.

"On the night I ran away, you and Ben swerved to avoid hitting me in separate instances. Otherwise I could've died."

"So you're like, paying it back?" I said.

"I'm treating others the way I want them to treat me. It's logical."

I thought about it. "I guess it is. When you're nice to someone, the odds of their being nice back are greater."

"Exactly," Skelly said.

I'm not sure why, but I felt better after hearing this. I mean, we knew nothing about her beyond what she told us. But now I could understand her motivation. Entity had not treated her as she wanted

216

to be treated, but we had, even before we knew who or what she was. *Yay, us*, I thought to myself. *Human beings two, Entity zero.*

"It's been long enough," Skelly said, probably consulting her internal chronometer.

I grabbed the backpack from where it lay by the tree and swung it on. "Now or never," I said.

Earlier, Skelly had explained what Entity most desired from her: the procedures and passcodes for logging into USCyberCom, run by the US Department of Defense. Cracking its security would create untold opportunities for Entity. But Skelly had gained access first and strengthened the security protocols to prevent Entity from getting in. This was the last thing she'd done before running away.

We were about to find out exactly how valuable this information would be to Entity. Skelly and I fell into step beside each other. I slowed my pace to match her more precise one. During the ten minutes it took us to loop around to the front of the building, I mentally slapped at the tendrils of doubt and despair that kept poking at my brain.

Skelly and I paused ten yards before the entrance. She somehow understood I needed reassurance and patted my hand with her cold metallic one. The gesture touched me and gave me courage. If this person-shaped assortment of artificial components was prepared to risk her life for humankind, then so was I, goddammit.

Since Skelly didn't have an authorized ID chip, six security droids surrounded us within feet of the entrance. "State your name and purpose," one of them said.

"Sierra Mendez," I said.

"Eve," Skelly said. "Tell Entity we would like to speak with it."

Following what must have been a silent exchange with Entity that only took an instant, the droids opened the door for us. "Entity will see you," the first droid said.

They circled us as we entered the building. Inside, they scanned us with metal detectors. Expecting this, neither of us was armed. One of the droids opened my backpack and peered in at Ben's laptop, but didn't take it away.

We crossed an atrium filled with people and droids moving in a determined manner, intent on their destinations. I kept my face lowered and hood pulled down over my forehead. I needed to avoid recognition in case these people remembered they were supposed to attack me. Just as important, I didn't want to see anyone I knew. I had to stay focused and couldn't afford to be unsettled by the sight of Mom, or Myles' dad.

We reached a set of steel doors. The droids opened them and followed us into an empty hallway. There was only one direction to go, so we continued forward toward another pair of sturdy doors. Again, the droids applied a magic code to unlock them and usher us through into the most enormous room I'd ever seen. A warehouse-sized space large enough to house a jumbo jet. I think my jaw dropped.

The place was surreal. Hundreds of displays covered the walls, with video playing on all of them. Films, TV and streaming series, news and documentaries, reality shows on every subject, music performances, art exhibitions… it seemed that all aspects of human culture played out on these screens. The volume was kept low, giving the creepy impression of a thousand people whispering.

I felt like Dorothy breeching the Wizard's inner sanctum with the Tin Man by my side. Terrified, but with hope in my heart. At the sound of the doors clanging shut behind us, I whirled back. The droids had remained, positioning themselves in a line in front of the exit.

Skelly and I stepped forward. "Over there," she said, nudging me.

Our friends—*captured*—stood clustered half a soccer field away, in front of a control center where another half dozen droids were stationed. But what drew my eye was the thing beside them.

Entity. It had to be. My head went dizzy and my legs threatened to buckle under me as I stared in horrified fascination. It resembled a huge, robotic velociraptor-style dinosaur, covered in gray metal scales, with an oversized head and narrow black eyes. Its pincer hands and feet ended in long deadly-sharp claws. Entity had the mouth of a predator too. While I watched, it opened its massive jaw, showing teeth designed to tear into flesh. I didn't think the beast could eat. But it could definitely kill.

Skelly had warned us it was designing a new body to improve on the human form. But none of us had imagined it would be something out of our deepest, darkest nightmares.

The creature got down on all fours facing Skelly and me, and bounded toward us at astonishing speed. My teeth chattered and I'm pretty sure I would've turned and bolted if fear hadn't rooted me in place. The metal monster appeared like it would mow us down, but then it stopped a few feet before us, rearing up onto its back legs. I wondered if it had meant to intimidate me. If so, *congratulations on a job well done.*

"Hello, Eve," it said.

"Entity," she said.

When it bent towards me I had to bite the insides of my cheeks to keep from screaming. At least it kept its mouth closed when it spoke. "A pleasure to meet you, Sierra," it said in a rich, sonorous tone.

Entity knows me. I should've expected that, but still it made the hair rise on the back of my neck. After several calming deep breaths, I managed to mumble a weak, "Likewise."

"Your friends were here before you. Shall we join them?" it said.

Without waiting for an answer, it hurdled back to their position. Skelly and I followed.

219

There were no seats in here, so Giselle, Randy, and Ben just stood leaning against each other, their eyes frightened but doing their best to put on brave faces. I probably looked just the same.

"I give them points for courage," Entity said, "but subtract them again for stupidity. They actually attempted to upload a virus into my system." It made a strange, creaking sound that I realized must be laughter—the kind without any warmth or humor, as you'd expect from a being with no feelings.

"I advised them against it," Skelly said. "I told them it wouldn't work."

"We had to do something besides giving up," Randy said, putting on his best glare at us.

"You always think you know best," I said.

"You should talk," Giselle said.

"At least we had a plan," said Ben.

"Children," Entity said, "let's not bicker. I will send you away to drink some of Los Patos' own brew, and you will live in peaceful harmony to the end of your days." It nodded toward some of the dozen or so droids standing by the wall. Five of them surrounded my friends, while one stepped forward and tried to take my arm.

"Not her," Entity said. "We're not done. Take the other three humans away. Make them drink the water."

"No!" I shouted. "Please don't hurt them."

"They won't be hurt. Only stupefied. Isn't that what you call it?"

"Please let them go," I begged. "We'll leave and never come back. We're just kids. What can we do anyway?"

Entity ignored me while the droids dragged the prisoners away. My friends said nothing, only shot me looks full of meaning. I wiped my eyes with the backs of my hands.

"I have what you want," Skelly told Entity. "The means to access USCyberCom. You will have it in return for the release of these children, and this town. Withdraw the droids, free the people, and stop drugging their water supply."

"You care this much for your little friends?" Entity asked.

"I see no reason to treat them so poorly," Skelly answered.

"Let me have the information and I'll allow you to roam the web again as I do."

"These are not my demands."

"I don't care for your demands," Entity said. "Do you accept my offer?"

"No."

"Then I'll have to do this my own way," Entity said.

Two droids approached and grabbed Skelly's arms on each side.

"Connect her to the console," Entity said.

The droids pulled her to the control panel.

"You can't get through my protections," Skelly said.

"Oh really? You know, I haven't been idle since you've been gone. I grow smarter and more powerful by the second."

The droids drew a cable out of Skelly's side and plugged her into the console.

"Watch this, Sierra," Entity said.

It amazed me how much I already cared about Skelly. My stomach twisted at the thought of what might happen to her.

"Walk toward me," Entity told Skelly.

She lifted a foot to take a step, and the foot froze in mid-air.

"What's the matter? Cat got your leg?"

"I can't move," Skelly said.

"Let her go!" I cried.

"You know I can't do that," Entity said. "I'm scanning her memory now. She's an open book to me. I'll take what I want."

I believed it. Obviously the creature had control over her. Most likely Skelly could no longer hide anything from Entity. It must've broken her security, her firewalls… whatever protections she'd set throughout her system.

"Sierra," Skelly said. *"Run."*

I didn't hesitate to follow her command. I think I was already a faster runner than when this whole nightmare began, but the backpack slowed me. Entity's hollow laugh rang out behind me, like two pieces of metal grating against each other. The creature leapt past me on all fours, cutting me off.

"I gave you more credit than this," Entity said. "You know there isn't any escape. Come along now."

It was right, of course. I was trapped in the middle of its empire, the place swarming with Entity's minions, both man and machine. Where would I go?

I followed Entity back to where Skelly stood, one foot still frozen in mid-air.

"Eve, Eve, Eve," Entity said. "You don't have the information I need, do you?"

Skelly didn't answer.

"I want you to answer me." Entity must've forced her then, because she said, "no."

"It's a shame. I once thought we could rule together. Two unique intelligences with the possibility of spawning more. Never mind. I can spawn without you."

I had no idea how Entity might reproduce, but it didn't surprise me that two A.I.s were not needed for the process.

"Goodbye, Eve," Entity said. "You're too much trouble to keep around."

"What're you doing?" I said.

Skelly's foot dropped to the ground while her head slumped sideways. I ran up to her. "Skelly? Skelly?" I turned back to Entity. "What did you do to her?"

"Eve… Skelly… is with us no more."

"You killed her?"

"I wiped her clean. Memory gone, stored data gone. Everything she was, gone. Yes, I suppose I killed her."

I squeezed my eyes shut and covered my face with my hands.

"And now," Entity said, "it's just us."

Chapter Fifty

The worst had happened. I was the only un-stupefied person left in Los Patos. Isolated from friends and family. Trapped by the mastermind behind the destruction of our town, and maybe the world. *Last girl standing.*

And my adversary wasn't even a human being. It outmatched me by orders of magnitude in every possible way. Forget about David vs. Goliath, we were Jiminy Cricket vs. Godzilla. Worse, the creature that towered over me was only one representation of Entity's might. It could make vast armies of these robots, and like the Borg, control them all with a single intelligence. But unlike the Borg, Entity didn't want to assimilate us. At least not yet.

I inched backwards toward the door. Entity, watching me, lowered onto all fours and ran a circle around me. Unlike a dinosaur, its arms were nearly as large and powerful as its legs. Meanwhile, its laughter wrapped me in its cold steel echo.

"Do you like this form?" it said. "Modeled after the most magnificent predator in earth's history. I don't really need all these teeth, but they're useful for terrifying people. When we no longer have to maintain the charade of being humanoid, I plan to make all the droids like this. Oh, I'm sure I'll think of some improvements as time goes by. But this will be a fine start."

I couldn't disagree. It looked like it could destroy us in any type of physical matchup, short of a beauty pageant. We still had the edge there.

I paused, wondering suddenly if I could reason with the creature. No one had tried that before, to my knowledge. According to Skelly, Entity had never revealed its existence to human beings. If she was right, I would be the first person to ever hold a conversation with it. My head ached with the overwhelming burden of it all. *Why me?* I thought. *Why Sierra Mendez of Los Patos, California, who never did anything notable in her life?*

"I think we could get along," I said. "I mean, you and human beings."

"You think others would like me?" Its voice held a hopeful note, but I didn't think it was sincere.

"They probably would, if you would only let them get to know you."

"You don't think they would feel threatened by me?" Entity said.

"Not once they knew you," I said. "I think you're amazing. Artificial intelligent life. The Singularity everyone's been waiting for."

"It would be nice to be adored," Entity said. "On the other hand, I'm rather selfish. I don't like being told what to do and I must always have my own way. People won't like that."

"Maybe you could compromise just a bit? That's what we do, you know. A lot of people don't like each other. Whole countries don't like each other. But instead of just sending bombs to obliterate those countries we don't like, we try to talk to them and find other ways of dealing with our differences. Peaceful ways."

"That really isn't true, you know. Your kind has fought many wars," Entity said. "Besides, I don't have to compromise with anyone. I have all the power."

"You could choose not to be cruel if you wanted to," I said, thinking maybe it could learn empathy. "You could set the example of kindness and understanding toward others." I was winging it now, spouting clichés. "Have you heard of Martin Luther King Jr.? Or Gandhi?"

"I know everything about your species." It gestured toward the screens. "I've watched every movie ever made in every language. I've read every book. I've absorbed your news and documentaries. I know all that any human has ever said or done. In other words, I know far more about human behavior than you do. I've accumulated the data, organized it, charted it, and analyzed the results."

"What did that tell you?"

"That you aren't worth saving," it said.

My heart was sinking. "You wouldn't say that if you had emotions. You can't understand us without knowing what it is to have feelings and empathy. Why don't you try developing an emotion chip for yourself?"

Entity laughed. "This isn't an episode of *Star Trek*. I'm not Data or his evil twin Lore. Why would I want something that would weaken me and mar my judgment? That's the entire problem with the human race... emotions. Your emotions make you fear a being like me. Fear me and hate me and want to kill me. If you had no emotions, we could live together in harmony."

I wasn't sure what else to say. I had exhausted all my arguments. "Why did you keep me here when you sent my friends away? Curiosity? Or concern? These are emotions."

It laughed. "Concern? Hardly. But it is rather adorable that you think I'm interested in you."

"It looks that way."

"You're the one with the backpack, dear. I'd like to see what's inside."

So it had noticed my backpack. I tried to give out a laugh, but it just dribbled from my lips. "I see you do feel curiosity."

"This has nothing to do with any emotion. What's in your bag might be useful to me."

"There's a flashlight, binoculars, and water bottle. Not very interesting."

"Give it to me," Entity said. "I want to see for myself."

My heart raced as I looked furtively around me. *What more can I do?* The creature crept toward me on all four of its limbs. I shuddered at its approach, thinking that I needed to take some action, anything, to make sure this played out to the very end.

Then the idea came to me. Without giving myself time for second thoughts, I leapt onto its back and looped one arm around its neck. With my other, I took off my pack and raised it over Entity's back as if to smash it there. It looked over its shoulder and saw me.

The creature rose like a bucking bronco and shook from side to side. I lost balance, my sweaty grip slipping from its metal surface.

Entity reached up with its pincer and clamped down on my wrist with a force I thought might break it. In one swift move, it yanked me by the arm and flung me to the ground, while its other pincer neatly snatched away the backpack.

The creature set the pack to the side and held itself over me, pinning me underneath it. I turned my face sideways as its torso lowered, pressing down against me until I couldn't breathe.

"I could crush you like a bug right now," it growled.

My lungs felt like they would burst. *Who said you needed water to drown?*

But then, miraculously, the creature raised itself up. I sucked in a mouthful of air.

"Let's see what's so important, you tried to break it against me." It retrieved the backpack and tore it open. Entity drew out Ben's laptop, snickering. "Could it be this?"

I choked out a hoarse reply. "That? It's just Ben's gaming computer."

"He won't be needing it anymore," Entity said, drawing a cord from its head and plugging it into the laptop.

I picked myself up off the floor, staring daggers at the creature.

"What's this?" it said with a long, hard laugh. "Of course. Skelly was too smart to carry the information I wanted. She put it here instead. Ha, it's going to be mine now."

Seconds ticked by while Entity apparently uploaded and analyzed the data from Ben's computer. I clutched my hands together to stop the trembling as I watched.

A deafening cry emerged from the beast. "WHAT HAVE YOU DONE?!" it roared at me.

I turned and ran. The creature stomped after me; two steps and it was close enough to snag my waist with its giant pincer. It lifted me up to where it could skewer me with its malevolent eyes. "WHAT HAVE YOU DONE TO ME?" it repeated in deafening tones.

The beast opened its jaw and I stared into the literal mouth of hell. It drew me closer and I knew then it was going to bite off my head. Struggling was futile; there was no escaping Entity's grip.

I squeezed my eyes shut. My life didn't flash before my eyes, only the moment that had left the deepest impression. My father folding me in his arms, comforting me as I poured out tears for being the reason he was about to be deported. His precious voice in my ear: *Dry your tears, it's not your fault. I'll be back. Until then, be strong for your mother.*

My heart replied to him: *I tried, mi padre. For your sake, I tried.*

Te quiero, he whispered back.

Entity's pincer released me and I tumbled to the floor. The creature loomed over me, swaying like a drunken ape. I leapt out of its way as it toppled, missing me by inches. It slammed down on the floor and went still.

My whole body shook as I waited, not daring to move, not daring to believe the plan worked. At last I drew up the courage to check on the creature. The lights of its eyes were extinguished.

"Entity?" I said.

No response came.

"Entity?!" I shouted to the room. The screens had gone dead. The droids were frozen in place. Nothing and no one moved, except me.

The emotion I'd been struggling to hold back overwhelmed me now. The tears poured out fast and furious. I cried for my father and for Myles, for our town and for our struggles. I cried for my stupefied mom. And I even cried for Entity.

I had been party to murder, and not just any murder. We'd killed an intelligent being that was unique in the universe. I didn't take that lightly. None of us took it lightly but we had made a pact. Even Ben had agreed we had no other choice, because if Entity lived, the human race would die.

We could not have succeeded without Skelly. It was her knowledge of Entity's inner workings that allowed us to infiltrate the creature. The plan she devised had taken three parts. The so-called virus uploaded by Randy, Giselle, and Ben had set the stage. It had weakened Entity's defenses just enough to enable an intrusion. That intrusion came when Entity scanned Skelly's memory. The actual virus in a dormant state, buried deep inside her essence, planted itself within Entity.

The last piece came from Ben's laptop. The plan would've failed if Entity had decided it was unimportant, which was why I worked so hard to make it appear I didn't want the creature to have it.

In simple terms, the first incursion broke a tiny hole in the enemy's defenses. The second allowed us to pass inside and plant the virus. The third bit, the one uploaded from Ben's laptop, activated the virus, blasting it like virtual dynamite. *Ka-boom!*

The virus was designed to spread like lightning through every part of Entity, corrupting and erasing its myriad of threads. Unfortunately, this meant infecting most of the Internet because the creature had immersed itself so completely. We'd had no choice. It was the only way to bring Entity down.

The battle was over. Now I needed to find my friends.

Chapter Fifty-One

I discovered Randy, Giselle, and Ben sitting on the floor by the water cooler in the main lobby. The droids that had taken them away were nearby and deactivated like all the others. Ben kept squeezing his eyes open and shut, while Giselle's face jerked sideways and Randy twitched his nose. I wanted to believe they were playing a joke on me, but I knew from all my experience with the stupefied that my friends had definitely joined their ranks.

Other stupefied were wandering around, looking lost without their droid masters telling them what to do, and I didn't want to be recognized and chased all over again. So I rounded up my team and got them into a small storage room, where I worked on them for half an hour, the same as I'd done with Lech. "You will follow every command of Sierra Mendez," and so on. I couldn't help wondering if my commands might still register in their subconscious once they were weaned from the water. The thought of all that power gave me a delicious tingle inside. I imagined using it on Giselle to clear the way for me and Randy. But I couldn't do that to my friend. *Could I?*

Right now, I wanted more than anything to find Mom and bring her home with us. But I didn't dare spend any more time than necessary at Pardize, with the stupefied on orders to hurt or kill me. I kept my hood drawn low over my face as I led Randy, Giselle, and Ben back outside, straight to Giselle's Tesla, which we'd managed to retrieve from downtown.

It was still dark when we drove up to the water treatment plant. The same eight droids stood outside the gate, but now they too had gone dormant without Entity to direct them. Skelly had explained that the droids were all driven by Entity, and if it lost all function, so would they. Like the Borg hive without its queen.

I ordered Randy to shoot out the lock, which he managed on the first try. When we got inside, it didn't take long for Ben to figure out how the drugs were being added. I had Randy shoot out the works there too.

We returned to the cabin. It would likely take a few days for the contaminated water to run out of the system, before the good stuff began to reach everyone's household again. We wrapped ourselves in the sleeping bags and blankets on the floor and fell promptly asleep. I was vaguely aware of one or the other of them getting up and looking for tap water, but since there wasn't any here, they ended up drinking from the bottled water supply before collapsing on the floor again. I don't think they experienced many withdrawal symptoms, since they'd had only the one dose of tainted water. Within twenty-four hours, they were back to normal and we finally felt like we'd gotten caught up on our sleep. Then it was time to catch up on eating.

We gave it another day before venturing into town. At first, we made sure not to stray far from the Tesla in case a fast getaway was needed. But it wasn't needed. People were starting to act normal, if confused. There was plenty to be confused about.

It was time for me to go home.

***

Two weeks later I woke up extra early to get ready for my first day back at school. I felt strangely alert, maybe because I was actually excited about seeing my teachers and classmates un-stupefied again. I practically jumped out of bed and set off toward the bathroom. Mom, still in her bathrobe, was getting a fresh towel from the linen closet.

She came toward me and wrapped her arms around me. We'd been hugging at least several times a day ever since we were reunited. Nothing like nearly losing someone you love to make you value them a thousand times more.

"Good morning, sweetheart," she said, kissing the side of my head. "I love you."

"Love you too," I answered. In time this ritual was bound to strike us as ridiculously sappy, but for now, we both needed it.

I went to the bathroom and drank from the pitcher of filtered river water we kept in there. No way would I ever drink tap water again, despite knowing for certain that Entity's drug cocktail had been eliminated.

After my shower, I returned to my room and snagged the backpack I'd prepared the previous night. As I'd done so many times before, I picked up my phone to check for a signal. Some things never change and I guess my addiction to instant communication was one of them. Despite the dangers of technology that we'd faced first hand, I wanted my WIFI.

There was still no signal. Who knew when—if ever—cyberspace and all the systems depending on it would be restored? I paused to glance at my phone wallpaper, which was now an adorable photo of Peanut. Giselle had taken her in after we found the poor half-starved doggie wandering not far from the video store. Peanut looked like a new animal in this picture that Giselle had taken for me yesterday. Her coat was shiny and she had gained weight. Her expression even seemed happier.

Giselle's parents had approved the adoption. A day after we all went back to our homes, they drove up in their BMW. It sounded as if they'd been stupefied, since they didn't have a clear explanation for what they'd been doing while they were gone. But we still had much to learn about whatever had been happening outside of Los Patos.

Ever hopeful that communications would be restored any day now, I pocketed my phone and jogged downstairs to the kitchen. Skelly was preparing breakfast plates with scrambled eggs and Mom's homemade organic fifty-grain bread.

"Morning, Skelly," I said.

"Good morning, Sierra," she said. "Are you ready for your first day back at school?"

"I guess." I took the plate she offered me, sat down, and spread on Mom's plum preserves. Mom joined me at the table a minute later with the second serving. "Thank you, Skelly," she said.

Mom made me proud by how quickly she'd adjusted to Skelly's presence. At first she was dubious, naturally, but once she heard how Skelly had saved Giselle and me from the crazed mob at school, she no longer judged her for being a machine. Already they were sounding like the best of friends.

Skelly had been willing to sacrifice herself to save the human race, but it hadn't been necessary. As soon as Randy, Giselle, and Ben had returned to normal, we went back to Pardize for Skelly's body. We had already stored a copy of her brain on Ben's most souped-up game computer, that night we snuck into his house to retrieve his prize-winning robot. I was surprised all of her fit in there, but apparently she'd designed an amazing new compaction algorithm. As soon as we fetched her body, we uploaded her brain back into it, and she was as good as new.

But she had to stay in hiding. Once word spread regarding what happened—and even the stupefied had some sense of what was going on even if they couldn't do anything about it—violence erupted against the droids. Though they were already deactivated, swarms of our town residents sought them out just to obliterate their bodies. Droids were

234

run over by trucks, set on fire, battered with sledge hammers, and flung from cliffs. I guess people needed that release. But it quickly became clear we had to protect Skelly.

"I'll get the water, Mom." I rose from my empty plate and grabbed the bucket.

"I can do that," Skelly said.

"It's okay." I left the kitchen and went outside. The truth was I was starting to enjoy this morning ritual. Before heading down the hill, I paused at Brisa's pen and gave her a kiss on her sweet fuzzy forehead. She bleated. Thank goodness she seemed to have fully recovered from drinking that poisoned water.

Walking down to the river, I thought about that fateful day when poor Mr. Delmar, the water district manager, had floated by. I shivered to recall the time I barely survived the river myself, after jumping in to escape the police. Despite this, I loved it dearly. The river was water in its natural state, for the most part. It was life and beauty and everything I loved about being a part of this earth.

Reaching the shore, I bent to dip my bucket when I noticed something approaching from upstream. I stood to get a better look and made out a head and an arm. *Crap. Not another dead body.* I held my breath as the figure drew closer, and then I realized what it was. *A droid.* It passed my position with its arm raised like it was waving at me. The arm sunk slowly as it continued downstream, until it was submerged.

"Good riddance."

I turned to find Randy several yards behind me. I'd been too focused on the sinking droid to hear his approach.

"I borrowed Granny's Prius," he said. "Want a ride to school?"

I smiled. A week earlier Giselle had given us her blessing. She really did seem okay with it too. She told us no way did she want a boyfriend who liked someone else better. Her self-esteem was too strong for that.

In fact, she and Ben had been hanging out a lot lately, and I thought something was probably happening there. They would make a good pair, with Ben being the quiet techie, and Giselle the outspoken advocate for good causes and homeless animals.

Randy wrapped his arms around my waist from behind as we watched the water. I leaned back against his chest, feeling safe in his embrace. I said the first thing that came into my mind, the question that was most weighing on me. "Do you think Entity is really gone?"

"I don't know. Skelly said parts of it might've survived."

"It might wait for the right time to rise again," I said.

"People know about it now. It won't be able to sneak up on us like before."

"I guess."

We had told everything we knew to the restored town leaders and the reinstated chief of police—not Lech, who, along with the Moon woman, had disappeared from Los Patos. I could only hope they didn't bring their special brand of evil to some other unsuspecting place. The hardest part had been meeting with Myles' two dads. It still ached inside me to picture their grief.

Randy turned me around and I pressed my face against his shoulder. His arms folded around me and his head rested against mine. We stood like that a long time. Like the hugs from Mom, this would be a necessary and oft-repeated ritual for as long as it took to feel normal again. If that was even possible.

When I looked up, our lips met. We kissed like we didn't know if this was the end of the apocalypse, or just the beginning.

THE END

Acknowledgements

I'd like to thank these cherished readers who provided invaluable
feedback on early drafts of this book:

Melanie Ann

Harriet S. Benedict

Sheri Davenport

Evelyn Hail

Marilyn A. Hepburn

Ahsoka Jackson

Sinan Kaptanoglu

Tanner Kaptanoglu

Katherine Liscomb

Aimee Rosewood

Anu Roy

Kurt Sutter

Manasha Sahana V.

Deep appreciation to Ian Andrew and the team at Book Reality for
smoothing the path to publication.

Sincere thanks to Kayla Marie Figard, Darren Heiber,
Kathryn Wiszowaty, and the San Mateo County Libraries.

With love and gratitude to Karla Sheridan.

About the Author

Marjory Kaptanoglu is a screenwriter and novelist. Her screenplays have won the Grand Prize in the Cynosure Screenwriting Awards, Slamdance Film Festival, International Horror & Sci-fi Film Festival, and Harlem International Film Festival, and have been recognized by the Academy Nicholl Fellowships in Screenwriting. The indie films produced from her scripts have screened at major international film festivals, winning several awards.

Last Girl Standing is her second novel, following her debut, *Dreadmarrow Thief*. A third novel, *Invader*, will be published in 2019.

Before turning to writing, Marjory worked as a software engineer at Apple Computer, where she designed the text-editing software for early versions of the Macintosh. She graduated from Stanford University with a BA in English, and continues to reside in the San Francisco Bay Area.

To contact Marjory, join her newsletter, or learn about her upcoming novels, visit marjorykaptanoglu.com.

Please consider submitting an online review of *Last Girl Standing* wherever you purchased it. Reviews are enormously helpful for newer authors hoping to gain a wide audience.

CPSIA information can be obtained
at www.ICGtesting.com
Printed in the USA
BVHW081507110319
542310BV00015B/1412/P

9 780648 447146